# Dwellers In The Hills

*by*

Melville Davisson Post

Double9 BOOKS

# Dwellers In The Hills

## by Melville Davisson Post



ISBN: 978-93-70422-60-5

**Published by**

**DOUBLE 9 BOOKS**
2/13-B, Ansari Road
Daryaganj, New Delhi – 110002
info@double9books.com
www.double9books.com
Tel. 011-40042856

# ABOUT THE AUTHOR

Melville Davisson Post is an American writer who was born in Harrison County, West Virginia. Although his name may be unfamiliar to those outside of professional circles, several of his collections are still in print, and his contributions appear in many detective fiction anthologies. Uncle Abner, Post's most renowned character, is a West Virginia backwoodsman who solves mysteries and upholds justice. The 22 Uncle Abner stories, written between 1911 and 1928, have been termed "the finest mysteries ever written". Other regular characters include attorneys Randolph Mason and Colonel Braxton, as well as detectives Sir Henry Marquis and Monsieur Jonquelle. His usual output amounted to approximately 230 volumes, including some non-crime novels. Post was born on April 19, 1869 in Harrison County, West Virginia, as the son of rich farmer Ira Carper Post and Florence May (née Davisson). Post's ancestors arrived in the Clarksburg, West Virginia area in the late 18th century. Post earned his law degree from West Virginia University in 1892 and was elected to the Electoral College as the youngest member. He practiced law for a corporation in Wheeling, West Virginia, but became disillusioned in politics and instead focused on literature.

# CONTENTS

# CHAPTER I
# THE OCTOBER LAND

I sat on the ground with my youthful legs tucked under me, and the bridle rein of El Mahdi over my arm, while I hammered a copper rivet into my broken stirrup strap. A little farther down the ridge Jud was idly swinging his great driving whip in long, snaky coils, flicking now a dry branch, and now a red autumn leaf from the clay road. The slim buckskin lash would dart out hissing, writhe an instant on the hammered road-bed, and snap back with a sharp, clear report.

The great sorrel was oblivious of this pastime of his master. The lash whistled narrowly by his red ears, but it never touched them. In the evening sunlight the Cardinal was a horse of bronze.

Opposite me in the shadow of the tall hickory timber the man Ump, doubled like a finger, was feeling tenderly over the coffin joints and the steel blue hoofs of the Bay Eagle, blowing away the dust from the clinch of each shoe-nail and pressing the flat calks with his thumb. No mother ever explored with more loving care the mouth of her child for evidence of a coming tooth. Ump was on his never-ending quest for the loose shoe-nail. It was the serious business of his life.

I think he loved this trim, nervous mare better than any other thing in the world. When he rode, perched like a monkey, with his thin legs held close to her sides, and his short, humped back doubled over, and his head with its long hair bobbing about as though his neck were loose-coupled somehow, he was eternally caressing her mighty withers, or feeling for the play of each iron tendon under her satin skin. And when we stopped, he glided down to finger her shoe-nails.

Then he talked to the mare sometimes, as he was doing now. "There is a little ridge in the hoof, girl, but it won't crack; I know it won't crack." And, "This nail is too high. It is my fault. I was gabbin' when old Hornick drove it."

On his feet, he looked like a clothes-pin with the face of the strangest old child. He might have been one left from the race of Dwarfs who, tradition said, lived in the Hills before we came.

His mare was the mother of El Mahdi. I remember how Ump cried when the colt was born, and how he sat out in the rain, a miserable drenched rat, because his dear Bay Eagle was in the mysterious troubles of maternity, and because she must be very unhappy at being on the north side of the hill among the black hawthorn bushes, for that was a bad sign—the worst sign in the world—showing the devil would have his day with the colt now and then.

I used, when I was little, to hear talk once in a while of some very wonderful person whom men called a "genius," and of what it was to be a genius. The word puzzled me a good deal, because I could not understand what was meant when it was explained to me. I used to ponder over it, and hope that some day I might see one, which would be quite as wonderful, I had no doubt, as seeing the man out of the moon. Then, when El Mahdi came into his horse estate and our lives began to run together, I would lie awake at night trying to study out what sort of horse it was that deliberately walked off the high banks along the road, or pitched me out into the deep blue-grass, or over into the sedge bushes, when it occurred to him that life was monotonous, tumbling me upside down like a girl, although I could stick in my brother's big saddle when the Black Abbot was having a bad day,—and everybody knew the Black Abbot was the worst horse in the Hills.

Wondering about it, the suggestion came that perhaps El Mahdi was a "genius." Then I pressed the elders for further data on the word, and studied the horse in the light of what they told me. He fitted snug to the formula. He neither feared God, nor regarded man, so far as I could tell. He knew how to do things without learning, and he had no conscience. The explanation had arrived. El Mahdi was a genius. After that we got on better; he yielded a sort of constructive obedience, and I lorded it over him, swaggering like a king's governor. But deep down in my youthful bosom, I knew that this obedience was only pretended, and that he obeyed merely because he was indifferent.

He stood by while I hammered the stirrup, with his iron grey head held high in the air, looking away over the hickory ridge across the blue hills, to the dim wavering face of the mountains. He was almost seventeen hands high, with deep shoulders, and flat legs trim at the pastern as a woman's ankle, and a coat dark grey, giving one the idea of good blue steel. He was entirely, I may say he was abominably, indifferent, except when it came into his broad head to wipe out my swaggering arrogance, or when he stood as now, staring at the far-off smoky wall of the Hills, as though he hoped to find there, some day farther on, a wonderful message awaiting him, or some friend whom he had lost when he swam Lethe, or some ancient enemy.

I finished with the stirrup, buckled it back into its leather and climbed into the saddle. It was one of the bitter things that my young legs were not long enough to permit me to drive my foot deep into the wide, wooden stirrup and swing into the saddle as Jud did with the Cardinal, or as my brother did when the Black Abbot was in a hurry and he was not. I explained it away, however, by pointing out, like a boy, not that my legs were short, but that El Mahdi, the False Prophet, was a very high horse.

Jud had not dismounted, and Ump was on the Bay Eagle like a squirrel, by the time I had fairly got into the saddle. Then we started again in a long, swinging trot, El Mahdi leading, the Cardinal next, and behind him the Bay Eagle. The road trailed along the high ridge beside the tall shell-bark hickories, now the granary of the grey squirrel, and the sumach bushes where the catbirds quarrelled, and the dry old poplars away in the blue sky, where the woodpecker and the great Indian hen hammered like carpenters.

The sun was slipping through his door, and from far below us came a trail of blue smoke and a smell of wood ashes where some driver's wife had started a fire, prepared her skillet, and moved out her scrubbed table,—signs that the supper was on its way, streaked bacon, potatoes, sliced and yellow, and the blackest coffee in the world. Now and then on the hillside, in some little clearing, the fodder stood in loose, bulging shocks bound with green withes, while some old man or half-grown lad plied his husking-peg in the corn spread out before him, working with the swiftness and the dexterity of a machine, ripping the husk with one stroke of the wooden peg bound to his middle finger, and snapping the ear at its socket, and tossing it into the air, where it gleamed like a piece of gold.

Below was the great, blue cattle land, rising in higher and higher hills to the foot of the mountains. The road swept around the nose of the ridge and plunged into the woods, winding in and out as it crawled down into the grass hills. The flat curve at the summit of the ridge was bare, and, looking down, one could see each twist of the road where it crept out on the bone of the hill to make its turn back into the woods.

As I passed over the brow of the ridge, I heard Jud call, and, turning my head, saw that both he and Ump were on the ground, looking down at the road below. Jud stood with his broad shoulders bent forward, and Ump squatted, peering down under the palm of his hand. I rode back just in time to catch the flash of wheels sweeping into the wood from one of the bare turns of the road. Yet even in that swift glimpse, I thought I knew who was below, and so I did not ask, but waited until they should come into the open space again farther down. I sat with the bridle rein loose on El Mahdi's neck and my hands resting idly on the horn of the saddle. I think I must have been smiling, for when Ump looked up at me, his wizened face was so serious that I burst out into a loud laugh.

"Well," I said, "it's Cynthia, isn't it? At half a mile she oughtn't to be so very terrible." And I opened my mouth to laugh again. But that laugh never came into the world. Just then a big horse with a man's saddle on him and the reins tied to the horn trotted out into the open, and behind him Cynthia's bay cob and her high, trim cart, and beside Cynthia on the seat was a man.

I saw the red spokes of the wheel, the silver on the harness, the flash of the grey feather in Cynthia's hat, and even the bit of ribbon half-way out the long whip-staff. Then they vanished again, while up the wind came a peal of laughter and the rumble of wheels, and the faint hammering of horses in the iron road. On the instant, my heart gave a great thump, and grew very bitter, and my face hardened and clouded. "Who was it, Jud?" I said. And my jaws felt stiff. "It was surely Miss Cynthia," he began, "an' it was surely a Woodford cattle-horse." Then he stopped with his mouth open, and began to rub his chin. I turned to Ump. "What Woodford?" I asked.

The hunchback twisted his shaggy head around in his collar like a man who wishes to have a little more air in his throat. Then he said: "He was a big, brown horse with a bald face, an' he struck out with his knees when he trotted. Them's the Woodford horses. The saddle was black with long skirts, an' it had only one girth. Them's the Woodford saddles. An' the stirrups was iron, an' there are only one Woodford who rides with his feet in iron."

I looked at Jud, searching his face for some trace of doubt on which to hang a little hoping, but it was all bronze and very greatly troubled. Then he saw what I wanted, and began to stammer. "May be the horse was tender, an' that was the reason." But Ump piped in, scattering the little cloud, "That horse ain't lame. He trots square as a dog."

Jud looked away and swung up in his saddle. "May be," he stammered, "may be the horse throwed him, an' that was the reason." Again Ump, the destroyer of little hopes, answered from the back of the Bay Eagle, "No horse ever throwed Hawk Rufe."

I sucked in the air over my bit lips when Ump named him. Rufe Woodford with Cynthia! I thought for an instant that I should choke. Then I kicked my heels against El Mahdi and swung him around down-hill. He galloped from the jump, and behind him thundered the Cardinal, and the Bay Eagle, with her silk nostrils stretched, jumping long and low like a great cat.

# CHAPTER II
# THE PETTICOAT AND THE PRETENDER

Not least among the things which the devil's imps ought to know from watching the world is this: that hatred is always big when one is young. Then, if the heart is bitter, it is bitter through and through. It is terribly just, and terribly vindictive against the stranger who hurts us with a cruel word, against our brother when we have misunderstood his heart, against the traitor who owes us love because we loaned him love. It is strange, too, how that hatred becomes a great force, pressing out the empty places of the heart, and making the weak, strong, and the simple, crafty.

El Mahdi ran with his jaws set on the bit, jumping high and striking the earth with his legs half stiff, the meanest of all the mean whims of this eccentric horse. On the level it was a hard enough gait; and on the hill road none could have stood the intolerable jamming but one long schooled in the ugly ways of the False Prophet. Along the skirts of the saddle, running almost up to the horn, were round, quilted pads of leather prepared against this dangerous habit. I rode with my knees doubled and wedged in against the pads, catching the terrible jar where there was bone and tendon and leather to meet and break it, and from long custom I rode easily, unconscious of my extraordinary precautions against the half-bucking jump.

The fence rushed past. The trees, as they always do, seemed to wait until we were almost upon them, and then jump by. Still the horse was not running fast. He wasted the value of his legs by jumping high in the air like a goat, instead of running with his belly against the earth like every other sensible horse whose business is to shorten distance.

He swept around the bare curves with the most reckless, headlong plunges, and I caught the force of the great swing, now with the right, and now with the left knee, throwing the whole weight of my body against the horse's shoulder next to the hill. Once in a while the red nose of the Cardinal showed by my stirrup and dropped back, but Jud was holding his horse well and riding with his whole weight in the stirrups and the strain on the back-webbed girth of his saddle where it ought to be. It was a dangerous road if the horse fell, only El Mahdi never fell, although he sometimes blundered like a cow; and the Cardinal never fell when he ran, and the Bay Eagle, who knew all that a horse ever learned in the world,—we would as soon have expected to see her fly up in the air as to fall in the road.

We were a mile down the long hill, thundering like a drove of mad steers, when I caught through the tree-tops a glimpse of Cynthia's cart, and wrenched the bit out of El Mahdi's teeth. He was not inclined to stop, and plunged, ploughing long furrows in the clay road. But a stiff steel bit is an unpleasant thing with which to take issue, and he finally stopped, sliding on his front feet.

We turned the corner in a slow, deliberate trot, and there, as calmly as though it were the most natural thing in the world, was Cynthia, sitting as straight as a sapling on the high seat, with the reins held close in her left hand, and beside her Woodford, and jogging along before the cart was the bald-faced cattle-horse.

A pretty picture in the cool shade of the golden autumn woods. Of course, Cynthia was the most beautiful woman in the world. My brother thought so, and that was enough for us. It was true that Ward observed her from a point of view wonderfully subject to a powerful bias, but that was no business of ours. Ward said it, and there the matter ended. If Ward had said that Cynthia was ugly, a trim, splendid figure, brown hair, and a manner irresistible would not have saved Cynthia from being eternally ugly so far as we were concerned; and although Cynthia had lands and Polled-Angus cattle and spent her winters in France, she must have remained eternally ugly.

So, when we knew Ward's opinion, from that day Cynthia was moved up to the head of the line of all the women we had ever heard of, and there she remained.

Our opinion of Woodford was equally clear. In every way he was our rival. His lands joined ours, stretching from the black Stone Coal south to the Valley River. His renters and drivers were as numerous and as ugly a set as ours.

Besides, he was Ward's rival among the powerful men of the Hills, ten years older, shrewd, clear-headed, and in his business a daring gambler. Sometimes he would cross the Stone Coal and buy every beef steer in the Hills, and sometimes Ward bought. It was a stupendous gamble, big with gain, or big with loss, and at such times the Berrys of Upshur, the Alkires of Rock Ford, the Arnolds of Lewis, the Coopmans of Lost Creek, and even the Queens of the great Valley took the wall, leaving the road to Woodford and my brother Ward. And when they put their forces in the field and man[oe] uvred in the open, there were mighty times and someone was terribly hurt.

I think Woodford lacked the inspiration and something of the swift judgment of my brother, but he stopped at nothing, and was misled by no illusions. Woodford and my brother never joined their forces. Ward did not trust him, and Woodford trusted no man on the face of the earth. There is an old saying that "the father's rival is the son's enemy"; and we hated Woodford with the healthy, illimitable hatred of a child.

I was young, and the arrogance of pride was very great as I pulled up by the tall cart. I had Cynthia red-handed, and wanted to gloat over the stammer and the crimson flush of the traitor. I assumed the attitude of the very terrible. Sharp and jarring and without premonition are the surprises of youth. This straight young woman turned, for a moment her grey eyes rested on the False Prophet and me, then a smile travelled from her red mouth out through the land of dimples, and she laughed like a blackbird.

"Of all the funny little boys! Dear me!" And she laughed again.

I know that the bracing influence of a holy cause has been tremendously overrated, for under the laugh I felt myself pass into a status of universal shrinking until I feared that I might entirely disappear, leaving a wonder about the empty saddle. And the blush and the stammer,—will men be pleased never to write in books any more, how these things are marks of the guilty? For here was Cynthia, as composed as the October afternoon, and here was I stammering and red.

"Quiller!" she pealed, "what a little savage! Do look!" And she put her grey glove on her companion's arm.

Woodford clapped his hand on his knee, and broke out into a jeering chuckle. "Why!" he said, "it's little Quiller. I thought it must be some bold, bad robber."

The jeer of the enemy helped me a little, but not enough. The reply went in a stammer. "You are all out of breath," said Cynthia; "a hill is no place to run. The horse might have fallen."

I gathered my jarred wits and answered. "Our horses don't fall." It was the justification of the horse first. Woodford stroked his clean-cut jaw, tanned like leather. "Your brother," he said, "tumbled out of the saddle some days ago. It is said his horse fell."

My courage flared. "Do you know how the Black Abbot came to fall?" I answered.

"An awkward rider, little Quiller," he said. "Is it a good guess?"

"You know all about it," I began, breaking out in my childish anger. "You know how that furrow as long as a man's finger got on the Black Abbot's right knee. You know—" I stopped suddenly. Cynthia's eyes were resting on me, and there was something in their grey depths that made me stop.

But Woodford went on. "My great aunt," he said, "was thrown day before yesterday, but she did not take to her bed over it. How is your brother?"

"Able to take care of himself," I said.

"Perhaps," he responded slowly, "to take care of himself." And he glanced suggestively at Cynthia.

The innuendo was intolerable. I gaped at the slim, brown-haired girl. Surely she would resent this. Traitor if she pleased, she was still a woman. But she only looked up wistfully into Woodford's face and smiled as artless, winning, merry a smile as ever was born on a woman's mouth.

In that instant the picture of Ward came up before me. His pale face with its black hair framed in pillows; his hand, always so suggestive of unlimited resource, lying on the white coverlid, so helpless that old Liza moved it in her great black palm as though it were a little child's; and across on the mantle shelf, where he could see it when his eyes were open, was that old picture of Cynthia with the funny little curls.

I felt a great flood rising up from the springs of life, a hot, rebellious flood of tears. A moment I held them back at the gateway of the eyepits, then they gushed through, and I struck the False Prophet over his iron grey withers, and we passed in a gallop.

# CHAPTER III
# THE PASSING OF AN ILLUSION

El Mahdi wanted to run, and I let him go. The swing of the horse and the rush of fresh, cool air was good. Nothing in all the world could have helped me so well. The tears were mastered, but I had a sense of tremendous loss. I had jousted with the first windmill, riding up out of youth's golden country, and I had lost one of the splendid illusions of that enchanted land. I was cruelly hurt. How cruelly, any man will know when he recalls his first jamming against the granite door-posts of the world.

Of love and all its mysterious business, I knew nothing. But of good faith and fair dealing I had a child's conception, the terrible justness of which is but dimly understood. The new point of view was ugly and painful. From the time when I toddled about in little dresses and Ward carried me on his shoulder in among the cattle or hoisted me up on the broad horn of his saddle, I had looked upon him as a big, considerate Providence. I did not understand how there could be anything that he could not do, nor anything in the world worth having at all that he could not get, if he tried. So when he told me of Cynthia, I considered that she belonged to us, and passed on to the next matter claiming my youthful attention. It never occurred to me that Cynthia could be other than happy to pass under the suzerainty of my big brother. True, I never thought very much about it, since it was so plainly a glorious privilege. Still, why had she made her promise, if she could not keep her shoulder to it like a man? We did not like it when Ward told us. We did not think much of women, Ump and Jud and I, except old Liza, who was another of those splendid Providences. Now it was clear that we were right.

It all went swimmingly when Ward was by, but no sooner was he stretched out with a dislocated shoulder from that mysterious blunder of the Black Abbot, than here was Cynthia trailing over the country with Hawk Rufe.

I stopped at the old Alestock mill where Ben's Run goes trickling into the Stone Coal, climbed down from El Mahdi and washed my face in the water, and then passed the rein under my arm and sat down in the road to await the arrival of my companions. The echo of the horses' feet was already coming, carried downward across the pasture land, and soon the head of the Cardinal arose above the little hill behind me, and then the Bay Eagle, and in a moment more Ump and Jud were sitting with me in the road.

We usually dismounted and sat on the earth when we had grave matters to consider. It was an unconscious custom like that which takes the wise man into the mountains and the lover under the moon. I think the Arab Sheik long and long ago learned this custom as we had learned it,—perhaps from a dim conception of some aid to be had from the great earth when one's heart is very deeply troubled.

I knew well enough that my companions had not passed Woodford without running the gauntlet of some interrogation, and I waited to hear what they had to say. I think it was Jud who spoke first, and his face was full of shadows. "I wouldn't never a believed it of Miss Cynthia," he began, "I wouldn't never a believed it."

"Don't talk about her," I broke in angrily. "What did Hawk Rufe say?"

Jud studied for a moment as though he were slowly arranging the proper sequence of some distant memory. Then he went on. "He wanted to know where I got that big red horse, an' if Mr. Ward's men ever walked any, an' he—" The man's open mouth closed on the broken sentence, and Ump answered for him, sitting under the Bay Eagle with his arm around her slim front leg. "An' he wanted to know what we did with little Quiller when he cried."

I thought I should die of the intolerable shame. I had cried—blubbered away as though I were a red-cheeked little girl in a clean calico petticoat.

After the dead line which Ump had crossed for him with the brutal frankness that went along with his dwarfed body, Jud continued with his report. "He asked me where we was goin', an' I told him we was goin' home. He asked me if we had had any word from Mr. Ward to-day, an' I told him we hadn't had any. Then he said we had better take the Hacker's Creek road because the Gauley was up from the mountain rains, an' runnin' logs, an' if we got in there in the night we would git you killed."

"An'," interrupted Ump, turning round under the Bay Eagle, "an' then Miss Cynthia looked up sharp at him like a catbird, an' she laughed, an' she said how that advice wasn't needed, because little boys always went home by the safest road."

The taunt sank in as oil sinks into a cloth. I may have blushed and stammered, and I may have blubbered like a milksop, but it was not because I was afraid. I would show Woodford and I would show this fickle Miss Gadabout that I did not need any advice about roads. If my life had been then in jeopardy, I would not have taken it burdened with a finger's weight of obligation to Rufus Woodford or Cynthia Carper. It might have gone out over the sill of the world, for good and all.

I arose and put the bridle rein over El Mahdi's head while I stood, my right hand reaching up on his high withers. Jud and Ump got into their saddles and turned down toward the ford of the Stone Coal on the Hacker's Creek road, which Woodford had suggested. But under the coat my heart was stewing, and I would not have gone that way if the devil and his imps had been riding the other. I climbed into the saddle and shouted down to them. They turned back at the water of the ford. "Where are you going?" I called.

"Home. Where else?" replied the dwarfed Ump.

"It's a nice roundabout way you're taking," I said. "The Overfield road is three miles shorter."

"But the Gauley's boomin'," answered Jud; "Woodford said not to go that way."

"It's the first time," I shouted, "that any of our people ever took directions from Hawk Rufe. As for me, I'm going by the Gauley." And I turned El Mahdi into the wooded road on the left of the turnpike.

For a moment the two hesitated, discussing something which I could not hear. Then they rode up out of the Stone Coal and came clattering after me.

It is wonderful how swiftly the night comes in among the boles of the great oak trees. The dark seems to rise upward from the earth. The sounds of men and beasts carry over long distance, drifting in among the trees, and the loneliness of the vast, empty earth comes back to us,—what is forgotten in the rush of the sunshine,—the constant loom of the mystery. One understands then why the early men feared the plains when it was dark, and huddled themselves together in the hills. Who could say what ugly, dwarfish things, what evil fairies, what dangerous dead men might climb up over the rim of the world? A man was not afraid of the grey wolf, or even the huge beast that trumpeted in the morass by the great water when the light was at his back, but when the world was darkened old men had seen strange shapes running by the wolf's muzzle, or groping with the big mastodon in the marsh land, and against these a stone axe was a little weapon.

Of all animals, man alone has this fear of the dark. Neither the horse nor the steer is afraid of shadows, and from these, as he travels through the night, a man may feed the springs of his courage. I have been scared when

I was little, stricken with panic when night caught me on the hills, and have gone down among the cattle and stood by their great shoulders until I felt the fear run off me like water, and have straightway marched out as brave as any trooper of an empress. And from those earliest days when I rode, with the stirrups crossed on my brother's saddle, after some kind old straying ox, I was always satisfied to go where the horse would go. He could see better than I, and he could hear better, and if he tramped peacefully, the land was certainly clear of any evil thing.

We crossed the long wooded hill clattering like a troop of the queen's cavalry, and turned down toward the great level bow which the road makes before it crosses the Gauley. There was a dim light rising beyond the flat lands where the crooked elves toiled with their backs against the golden moon. But they were under the world yet, with only the yellow haze shining through the door. This was the acre of ghosts. Tale after tale I had heard, sitting on the knee of the old grey negro Clabe, about the horrors of this haunted "bend" in the Gauley. There, when I was a child, had lived old Bodkin in a stone house, now a ruin, by the river,—a crooked, mean old devil with a great hump, and eyes like a toad. He came to own the land through some suspicious will about which there clung the atmosphere of crime, as men said. When I saw him first, I was riding behind my brother, and he stopped us and tried to induce Ward to buy his land. He was mounted on a red roan horse, and looked like an old knotty spider.

I can still remember how frightened I was, and how I hid my face against my brother's coat and hugged him until my arms ached. When Ward inquired why he wished to sell, he laughed in a sort of cackle, and replied that he was going to marry a wife and go to the moon.

Now, tradition told that he had married many a wife, but that they died quickly in the poisoned chamber of this spider. Ward looked the bridegroom over from his twisted feet to his hump, and there must have been some merry shadow in his face, for Bodkin leaned over the horn of his saddle and stretched out his hand, a putty-coloured hand, with long, bony fingers. "Do you see that?" he croaked. "If I ever get that hand on a woman, she's mine."

Then I began to cry, and Ward wished the old man a happy voyage to the cloud island, and we rode on.

He did marry a wife, and one morning, but little afterwards, two of my brother's drivers found her hanging to the limb of a dead apple tree with a bridle rein knotted to her neck, and her bare feet touching the tops of the timothy grass. When they came to look for Bodkin, he had disappeared with his red roan horse. Ward explained that he had ridden through the gap of the mountains into the South, but I thought, with the negroes, that someone ought to have seen him if he had gone that way; besides, I had heard him say that he was going to the moon. Later, old Bart and Levi Dillworth, returning from some frolic, had seen Bodkin riding his horse in a terrible gallop, with the dead woman across the horn of his saddle, on his way to the moon.

It was true that both Bart and Levi were long in the bow arm, and men who loved truth less than they loved laurels. Still the tale had splendid conditions precedent, and old Clabe arose to its support with many an eloquent wag of his head.

I was running through this very ghost story when El Mahdi stopped in the road and pricked up his ears. At the same moment Jud and Ump pulled up beside me. Perhaps their minds were in the same channel. We listened for full a minute. Far down in the marsh land I could hear the frogs chanting their mighty chorus to the stars, and the little screech-owl whining from some tree-top far up against the hill. I was about to ride on when Jud caught at the rein and put up his hand. Then I heard the sound that the horse was listening to, but at the great distance it was only a sound, a faint, wavering, indefinite echo, coming up from the far-away bend of the Gauley. The rim of the moon was rising now out of the under world, and I watched the road trailing away into a deep shadow by the river. As I watched, I saw something rise out of this gloom and sweep down the dim road. It passed for a moment through a belt of moonlight, and I saw that it was a horse ridden by a shadow.

Then we clearly heard long, heavy galloping. Jud dropped my rein and wrenched the Cardinal around on his haunches. He was not afraid of the living, but he was afraid of the dead. As the horse reared, Ump caught the bit under his jaw and, throwing the Bay Eagle against him, wedged the horse and Jud in between El Mahdi and himself. Ump was neither afraid of the living nor the dead. He called to me, and I seized the Cardinal's bit on my side, gripping the iron shank with my fingers through the rein rings.

Panic was on the giant Jud, and he lifted the horse into the air, dragging Ump and myself half out of our saddles. Men in their hopeless egotism have far underestimated the good sense of the horse. The Cardinal was in no wise frightened. At once, it seemed to me, he recognised the irresponsibility of his rider. In some moment of the struggle the bit slipped forward, and the horse clamped his powerful jaws on it and set the great muscles in his neck to help us hold.

The horses rocked and plunged, but we held them together. The Bay Eagle, quick-witted as any woman, crowded the Cardinal close, throwing her weight against his shoulders, and El Mahdi, indifferent, but stubborn as an ox, held his ground as though he were bolted to the road.

I heard Ump cursing, now Jud for his cowardice, now the ghost for its infernal riding. "Damn you, fool! Stay an' see it. Stay an' see it." And then, "Damn Bodkin an' his dead wife! If he rides this way, he stops here or he goes under to hell."

As for me, I was afraid. Only the swing and jamming of the struggle held me. The gallop of the advancing horse was now loud, clear, hammering like an anvil. It passed for a moment out of sight in a hollow of the road below. In the next instant it would be on us. The giant Jud made one last mighty effort. The Cardinal went straight into the air. I clung to the bit, dragged up out of the saddle. I felt my foot against the pommel, my knee against the steel shoulder of the great horse, my face under the Cardinal's wide red throat.

I heard the reins snap on both sides of the bit—pulled in two. And then the loud, harsh laugh of the man Ump.

"Hell! It's Jourdan an' Red Mike."

# CHAPTER IV
# CONCERNING HAWK RUFE

Old wise men in esoteric idiom, unintelligible to the vulgar, have endeavoured to write down in books how the human mind works in its house,—and I believe they have not succeeded very well. They have broken into this house when it was empty, and laboured to decipher the mystic hieroglyphics written on its walls, and learn to what uses the departed craftsman put the strange, delicate implements which they found fastened so primly in their places.

They have got at but little, as I have heard them say, deploring the brevity of life, and the tremendous magnitude of the labour. The learned, as one put it, had barely time to explain to his successor that he had found the problem unsolvable. I think they might as well have gone about tracking the rainbow, for all they have learned of this mysterious business.

In fewer moments than a singing maid takes to double back on her chorus, I had forgotten all about the ghost. I was sitting idly in the saddle now with the rein over my wrist. Jourdan's message from my brother had given enough to think of. I knew that Ward in the preceding autumn had bought the cattle of two great graziers south of the Valley River, to be taken up during the October month, but I did not know that on a summer afternoon he had sold these cattle to Woodford, binding himself to deliver them within three days after they were demanded.

The trade was fair enough when the two had made it. But now the price of beef cattle was off almost thirty dollars a bullock, and Woodford was in a position to lose more money than his bald-faced cattle-horse could carry in a sack. He had waited all along hoping for the tide to turn. Suddenly, to-day he had demanded his cattle.

To-day, when Ward was on his back and the cattle far to the south across the Valley River. It was the contract, and he had the right to do it, but it was like Woodford. Ward, helpless in his bed, had sent Jourdan on Red Mike to find us somewhere over the Gauley and bid us bring up the cattle if we could. And so the old man had ridden as though the devil were after him.

The proportions of Woodford's plan outlined slowly, and with it came a sense of tremendous responsibility. If we carried out the contract to the letter,—and to the letter it must be with this man,—I knew that Woodford would meet the loss, if it stripped the coat off of his shoulders,—meet it with a smile and some swaggering comment. And I knew as well that, if by any hook or crook he could prevent the contract from being carried out, he would do it with the devil's cleverness.

Only, I knew that the hand of Woodford would never rise against us in the open. We might be balked by sudden providences of God, planned shrewdly like those which a great churchman ruling France sometimes called to his elbow.

For such gentle business, not old Richelieu was better fitted with a set of arrant scoundrels. There was the cunning right hand of Hawk Rufe, the slick, villainous intriguer, Lem Marks. No diplomatic imp, serving his master in the kingdoms of the world, moved with more unscrupulous smoothness. There was Malan with his clubfoot, owned by the devil, the drovers said, and leased to Woodford for a lifetime. And there was Parson Peppers, singing the hymns of the Lord up the Stone Coal and down the Stone Coal. As stout a bunch of rogues as ever went trooping to the eternal bonfire, handy gentlemen to his worship Woodford.

It was preposterous overmatching for a child. Hawk Rufe had laughed well when I had heard him laughing last. If Ward were only back in the saddle of the Black Abbot! But he was stretched out over yonder with the night shining through his window, and there was on the turning world no one but me to strip to this duel.

Still, I had better horses, and perhaps better men than Woodford. Jud was one of the strongest men in the Hills, afraid of the dead, as I have written, but not afraid of any living thing on the face of the earth. They knew this over the Stone Coal; the club-footed giant Malan had a lot of scars under his shirt that were not born on him. And there was Ump, a crooked thing of a man truly, but a crooked thing of a man that would hobnob with the king of all the fiends, banter for banter, and in whose breast cowardice was as dead as Judas.

I looked down at the humble giant, shamefaced in the moonlight, tying his broken bridle reins back in their rings, and drawing the knots tight with his bronzed fingers that looked like the coupling-pins of a cart,—and then at the hunchback doubled up in his saddle. Maybe,—and my blood began to rise with it,—maybe when we looked close, the odds were not so terrible after all. Here was bone and sinew tougher than Malan's, and such cunning as might cry Marks a merrier run than he had gone for many a day.

Then, as by some sharp turn, I caught a new light on the two hours already gone. Man alive! We had been in the game for all of those two blessed hours with our eyes sealed up tight as the lid of a jar.

"How high was the Gauley?" I almost shouted, pointing my finger at Red Mike.

"'Mid sides," answered Jourdan, turning around in his saddle.

"'Mid sides!" I echoed; "and the logs? Was it running logs?"

"Nothin' but brush an' a few old rails. You can see the water mark on Red Mike right here at the bottom of the saddle skirt." And the old man reached down and put his finger on the smoking horse. "The Gauley ain't up to stop nothin'."

I clapped my teeth together. So much for the solicitous care of Hawk Rufe. If we had gone by the Hacker's Creek road we should have missed Jourdan and lost the good half of a day. Woodford knew that Ward would send by the shortest road. It was the first gleam of the wolf tooth shining for a moment behind the woolly face of the sheepskin.

I looked down at Ump. The hunchback put his elbow on the horn of his saddle and rested his jaw in the hollow of his hand.

"Old Granny Lanum," he said, "her that's buried back on the Dolan Knob, used to say that God saw for the little pup when it was blind, but after that it was the little pup's business. An' I reckon she knowed what she said."

Wiser heads than mine have pondered that problem since the world began its swinging,—but with greater elegance, but scarcely more clearly than Ump had put it. Old Liza used to tell me when I was very little that if I fought with those who were smaller than myself, I was fighting the wards of the Father in heaven, and it was a lot better to get a broken head from some sturdy urchin who was big enough to look out for himself. And I have always thought that old Liza was about as close to the Ruler of Events as any one of us is likely to get. Anyway I doubted not that if the good God rode in the Hills, He was far from stirrup by stirrup with Woodford.

Red Mike was beginning to shiver in his wet coat, and Jourdan gathered up his reins.

"Mr. Ward," he said, "told me to tell you to stay with old Simon Betts to-night, an' git an early start in the mornin'." Then he rode away, and we watched him disappear in the hollow out of which he had come carrying so much terror.

We were a sobered three as we turned back into the woods. Ghosts and all the rumours of ghosts had fled to the chimney corners. No witch rode and there walked no spirit from among the dead. Above us the oaks knitted their fantastic tops, but it made no fairy arch for the dancing minions of Queen Mab. The thicket sang, but with the living voices of the good crickets, and the owl yelled again, diving across the road, but his piping notes had lost their eerie treble.

There is something in the creak of saddle-leather that has a way of putting heart in a man. To hear the hogskin rubbing its yellow elbows is a good sound. It means action. It means being on the way. It means that all the idle talking, planning, doubting is over and done with. Sir Hubert has cut it short with an oath and a blow of his clenched hand that made the glasses rattle, and every swaggering cutthroat has his foot in the stirrup.

It is good, too, when one feels the horse holding his bit as a man might hold a child by the fingers. No slave this, but a giant ally, leading the way up into the enemy's country. Out of the road, weakling!

We travelled slowly back toward the Stone Coal. Far away a candle in some driver's window twinkled for a moment and was shut out by the trees. In the low land a fog was rising, a climbing veil of grey, that seemed to feel its path along the sloping hillside.

I heard the boom of the Stone Coal tumbling over the welts in its bedding as we turned down toward the old Alestock mill. The clouds had packed together in the sky, and the moon dipped in and out like a bobbin. As we swept into the turnpike by the long ford, Ump stopped, and, tossing his rein to Jud, slipped down into the road. El Mahdi stopped by the Cardinal. When I looked, the hunchback was on his knees.

"What are you doing?" I said.

Ump laughed. "I'm lookin' for hawks' feathers. Where they fly thick, there ought to be feathers."

He nosed around on the road for some minutes like a dog, and then disappeared over the bank into the willow bushes. The Stone Coal lay like a sheet of silver, broken into long hissing ridges, where it went driving over the ragged strata. On the other side, the Hacker's Creek road lifted out of the ford and went trailing away through the hills. In the moonlight it was a giant's ribbon.

I had no idea of what Ump was up to, but I should learn no earlier by a volley of questions. So I thrust my hands into my pockets and waited.

Presently he came clambering up the bank and got into his saddle.

"Well," I said; "did you find any feathers?"

"I did," he answered; "fresh ones from the meanest bird of the flock, an' he's flyin' low. I think that first turn into the Stone Coal fooled him. But he will know better by midnight."

Then I understood it was horse tracks he had been looking for.

"How do you know he's trailing us?" I asked.

"Quiller," he answered, "when Come-an'-go-fetch-it rides up an' down, he's lookin' for somethin'. An' I reckon we're are about ready to be looked for."

We were clattering up the turnpike while Ump was speaking. All at once, rising out of the far away hills, I heard a voice begin to bellow:

> "They put John on the island. Fare ye well, fare ye well.
> An' they put him there to starve him. Fare ye well, fare ye well."

It was Parson Peppers, and of his reverence be it said that no Brother of the Coast, rollicking drunk on a dead man's chest, ever owned a finer bellow.

I turned around in my saddle. "Peppers!" I cried. "Man alive! How did you know that it was the old bell-wether's horse?"

Ump chuckled. "I saw her shod once. A number six shoe an' a toe-piece."

# CHAPTER V
# THE WAGGON-MAKER

A spring of eternal youthfulness gushing somewhere under the bed of the mountains, was a dream of the Spanish Main, sought long and found not, as the legends run. But it is no dream that some of us carry our inheritance of youthfulness shoulder to shoulder with Eld into No Man's Country. Such an one was Simon Betts the waggon-maker.

I sat by his smouldering fire of shavings and hickory splinters, and wondered at the old man in the chimney corner. He was eighty, and yet his back was straight, his hair was scarcely grey, and his hands, resting on the arms of his huge wooden chair, were as unshrunken and powerful, it seemed to me, as the hands of any man of middle life.

Eighty! It was a tremendous hark back to that summer, long and long ago, when Simon came through the gap of the mountains into the Hills. The land was full of wonders then. The people of the copper faces prowled with the wolf and whooped along the Gauley. The Dwarfs lurked in the out-of-the-way corners of the mountains, trooping down in crooked droves to burn and kill for the very joy of doing evil. And who could say what unearthly thing went by when the wind shouted along the ridges? The folk then were but few in the Hills, and each busy with keeping the life in him. The land was good, broad waters and rich hill-tops, where the blue-grass grew though no man sowed it. A land made ready for a great people when it should come. With Simon came others from the south country, who felled the forest and let in the sunlight, and made wide pastures for the bullock, and so elbowed out the wandering and the evil.

High against the chimney, on two dogwood forks, rested the long rifle with its fishtail sight and the brass plate on the stock for the bullets and the "patching." Below it hung the old powder-horn, its wooden plug dangling from a string,—tools of the long ago. Closing one's eyes one could see the tall grandsires fighting in the beech forest, a brown patch of hide sighted over the brass knife-blade bead, and death, and to load again with the flat neck of the bullet set in the palm of the hand and covered with powder.

That yesterday was gone, but old Simon was doing with to-day. On two benches was a cart wheel, with its hickory spokes radiating like fingers from the locust hub, and on the floor were the mallet and the steel chisel with its tough oak handle. Stacked up in the corner were bundles of straight hickory, split from the butt of the great shell-bark log; round cuts of dry locust, and long timbers of white and red oak, and quarters of the tough sugars, seasoning, hard as iron. With these were the axe, the wedge, the dogwood gluts, and the mauls made with no little labour from the curled knots of the chestnut oak, and hooped with an iron tire-piece.

It was said on the country side that old Simon knew lost secrets of woodcraft taught by the early man;—in what moon to fell the shingle timber that it might not curl on the roof; on what face of the hill the sassafras root was red; how to know the toughest hickory by hammering on its trunk; when twigs cut from the forest would grow, if thrust in the earth; and that secret day of all the year when an axe, stuck into the bark of a tree, would deaden it to the root.

Simon Betts was not a man of many words. He smoked in the corner, stopping now and then to knock the ashes from his pipe, or to put some brief query. Jud and Ump had come in from the old man's log stable, throwing their saddles down by the door and spreading the bridles out on the hearth so that the iron bits would be warm in the morning.

"How will the day be to-morrow?" I asked of the waggon-maker.

"Dry," he responded; "great rains in the mountains, but none here for a week; then storms."

"Isn't it early for the storms?"

"Yes," he answered; "but the wild geese have gone over, and the storms follow."

Then he asked me where we were riding, and I explained that we were going to bring up Ward's cattle from beyond the Valley River. He said that we would find dry roads but high rivers. The gates of the mountains would be gushing with rains. The old man studied the fire.

Presently he said, "Mr. Ward is a good man. I have seen him buy a poor scoundrel's heifers and wink his eye when the scoundrel salted them the night before they were weighed, and then drove them to the scales in the morning around by the water trough."

I laughed. This was a trick originated long ago by one Columbus, an old grazing thief of the Rock Ford country, who went ever afterward by the name of "Water Lum." It was a terrible breach of the cattle code.

Again the old man relapsed into silence. His eyes ran over the shoulders of the big Jud who squatted by the fire, sewing his broken bridle reins with a shoemaker's wax-end.

"Are you the strong man?" he said.

The giant chuckled and grinned and drew out the end of his thread.

"Well," continued the waggon-maker, "Mr. Ward spoiled a mighty good blacksmith when he put you on a horse." Then he turned to me. "Is he the one that throwed Woodford's club-footed nigger in the wrastle at Roy's tavern?"

"Yes," I said, "but one time it was a dog-fall, and Lem Marks says that Malan slipped the other time."

"But he didn't slip," put in Jud. "He tried to lift me, an' I knee-locked him. Then I could a throwed him if he'd been as big as a Polled-Angus heifer."

"Was you wrastling back-holts or breeches-holts?" asked old Simon, getting up from his chair.

"Back-holts," replied Jud.

The waggon-maker nodded his head. Doubtless in the early time he had occasion to learn the respective virtues of these two celebrated methods.

"That's best if your back's best," he said; "but I reckon you ain't willing to let it go with a dog-fall. You might get another chance at him to-morrow. I saw him go up the road about noon."

Behind the old man Ump held up two fingers and made a sweeping gesture. The waggon-maker went back to the corner of his house for some bedding. Ump leaned over. "Two flyin'," he said. "One went east, an' one went west, an' one went over the cuckoo's nest. If I knowed where that cuckoo's nest was, we'd have the last one spotted."

"What do you think they're up to?" said I.

Ump laughed. "Oh ho, I think they're out lookin' for the babes in the woods!" And the fancy pleased him so well that he rubbed his hands and chuckled in his crooked throat until old Simon returned.

It was late, and the waggon-maker began his preparations for the night. He gave me a home-made mattress of corn husks and a hand-made quilt, heavy and warm as a fur robe. From a high swinging shelf he got two heifer hides, tanned with the hair on them, soft as cloth. In these Jud and Ump rolled themselves and, putting the saddles under their heads, were presently sleeping like the illustrious Seven. The old man fastened his door with a wooden bar, took off his shoes, and sat down by the fire.

I went to sleep with the picture fading into my dream,—the smoked rafters, the red wampus of the old waggon-maker, and the burning splinters crumbling into a heap of rosy ash. A moment later, as things come and go in the land of Nod, Cynthia and Hawk Rufe were also sitting by this fire. Cynthia held the old picture with the funny curls,—the one that stands on the mantel shelf at home,—and she was trying to rub out the curls with her thumb, moistening it in her red mouth. But somehow they would not rub out, and she showed the picture to Woodford, who began to count on his outspread fingers, "Eaney, meany, miny mo." Only the words were names somehow, although they sounded like these words.

Then the dream changed, and I was on El Mahdi in a press of fighting cattle, driven round and round by black Malan and Parson Peppers bellowing like the very devil.

When I awoke the fire was blazing and the grey light of the earliest dawn was creeping in through the chinks of the log wall. Ump and Jud had gone to the stable and the old waggon-maker was busy with the breakfast. On the hearth a mighty cake of corn-meal was baking itself brown; potatoes roasted in the ashes, and on a little griddle about as big as a man's hat a great cut of half-dried beef was broiling.

Famous chefs have spent a lifetime fitting beef for the royal table, and a king of France slighted the business of an empire for the acquirement of this art, and a king of England knighted a roast; but they all died and were buried without tasting beef as it ought to go into a man's mouth. I write it first. A Polled-Angus heifer, fed and watered and cared for like a child, should be killed suddenly without fright, and butchered properly; let the choice pieces hang from a rafter by green withes and be smoked with hickory logs until the fibres begin to dry in them, then cut down and broil.

I arose and went out of doors to wash the night off. Between the house and the log stable, under a giant sugar tree a spring of water bubbled out through the limestone stratum, ran laughing down a long sapling spout, and splashed into a huge old moss-covered trough.

With such food and such water, and the air of the Hills, is it any wonder that Simon Betts was a man at eighty? Hark ye! my masters of the great burgs, drinking poison in your smoky holes.

I plunged my head into the water, and my arms up to the elbows, then came out dripping and wiped it off on a homespun linen towel which the old man had given me when I left the house. As I stood rubbing my arms on the good linen, Ump and Jud came down from the stable and stopped to dip a drink in the long gourd that hung by the spring. They were about to pass on, when Ump suddenly stopped and pointed out a man's footprints leading from the stable path over the wet sod to the road. There were only one or two of these prints in the damp places below the spring, but they were fresh, and made by a foot smaller far than the wide one of old Simon Betts.

We followed Ump to the road. A horse had been hitched to the "rider" of the rail fence, and there were his tracks stamped in the hard clay. There was not light enough to see very clearly, so we struck matches and got down on the bank to study the details of the tracks. I saw that the horse had been one of medium size,—a saddle horse, shod with a "store" shoe, remodelled by some smith. But this knowledge gave no especial light.

Ump and Jud lay on their bellies with their noses to the earth searching the shoe marks. "It's no use," I said, "we can't tell." And I sat up. The two neither answered nor paid the slightest attention. No bacteriologist plodding in his eccentric orbit ever studied the outlines of a new-found germ with deeper or more painstaking care. Presently they began to compare their discoveries.

"He was a Hambletonian," began Jud; "don't you see how long the shoe is from the toe to the cork?" Ump nodded. "An' he was curbed," Jud went on; "his feet set too close under him fer a straight-legged horse. Still, that ain't enough."

"Put this to it," said the hunchback, "an' you've got your hand on him. Them's store nails hammered into a store shoe, an' the corks are beat squat. That's Stone's shoein'. Now you know him."

Then I knew him too. Lem Marks rode a curbed Hambletonian, and Stone was Woodford's blacksmith.

Jud got up and waved his great hand towards the south country.

"They're all ridin'," he said, "every mother's son of the gang. An' they know where we are."

"With rings on their fingers, an' bells on their toes," gabbled Ump; "an' we know where they are."

Then I heard the voice of the old waggon-maker calling us to breakfast.

# CHAPTER VI
# THE MAID AND THE INTRUDERS

There are mornings that cling in the memory like a face caught for a moment in some crowded street and lost; mornings when no cloud curtains the doorway of the sun; when the snaffle-chains rattle sharp in the crisp air and the timber cracks in the frost. They are good to remember when the wrist has lost its power and the bridle-fingers stiffen, and they are clear with a mystic clearness, the elders say, when one is passing to the ghosts.

It was such a morning when I stood in the doorway of the old waggon-maker's house. The light was driving the white fogs into the north. A cool, sweet air came down from the wooded hill, laden with the smell of the beech leaves, and the little people of the bushes were beginning to tumble out of their beds.

We asked old Simon if he had heard a horse in the night, and he replied that he had heard one stop for a few moments a little before dawn and presently pass on up the road in a trot. Doubtless, he insisted, the rider had dismounted for a drink of his celebrated spring water. We kept our own counsels. If the henchmen of Woodford hunted water in the early morning, it would be, in the opinion of Ump, "when the cows come home."

We went over every inch of the horses from their hocks to their silk noses, and every stitch of our riding gear, to be sure that no deviltry had been done. But we found nothing. Evidently Marks was merely spying out the land. Then we led the horses out for the journey. El Mahdi had to duck his head to get under the low doorway. It was good to see him sniff the cool air, his coat shining like a maid's ribbons, and then rise on his hind legs and strike out at nothing for the sheer pleasure of being alive on this October day. And it was good to see him plunge his head up to the eyepits into the sparkling water and gulp it down, and then blow the clinging drops out of his nostrils.

El Mahdi, if beyond the stars somewhere in those other Hills of the Undying I am not to find you, I shall not care so very greatly if the last sleep be as dreamless as the wise have sometimes said it is.

I spread the thick saddle-blanket and pulled it out until it touched his grey withers, and taking the saddle by the horn swung it up on his back, straightened the skirts and drew the two girths tight, one of leather and one of hemp web. Then I climbed into the saddle, and we rode out under the apple trees.

Simon Betts stood in his door as we went by, and called us a "God speed." Straight, honourable old man. He was a lantern in the Hills. He was good to me when I was little, and he was good to Ward. In the place where he is gone, may the Lord be good to him!

We stopped to open the old gate, an ancient landmark of the early time, made of locust poles, and swinging to a long beam that rested on a huge post in perfect balance. Easily pushed open, it closed of its own weight. A gate of striking artistic fitness, now long crumbled with the wooden plough and the quaint pack-saddles of the tall grandsires.

We rode south in the early daylight. Jud whistled some old song the words of which told about a jolly friar who could not eat the fattest meat because his stomach was not first class, but believed he could drink with any man in the Middle Ages,—a song doubtless learned at Roy's tavern when the Queens and the Alkires and the Coopmans of the up-country got too much "spiked" cider under their waistbands. I heard it first, and others of its kidney, on the evening that old Hiram Arnold bet his saddle against a twenty-dollar gold piece, that he could divide ninety cattle so evenly that there would not be fifty pounds difference in weight between the two droves, and did it, and with the money bought the tavern dry. And the crowd toasted him:

> "Here's to those who have half joes, and have a heart to spend 'em; But damn those who have whole joes, and have no heart to spend 'em."

On that night, in my youthful eyes, old Hiram was a hero out of the immortal *Iliad*.

We passed few persons on that golden morning. I remember a renter riding his plough horse in its ploughing gears; great wooden hames, broad breeching, and rusty trace chains rattling and clanking with every stride of the heavy horse; the renter in his patched and mud-smeared clothes,—work-harness too. A genius might have painted him and gotten into his picture the full measure of relentless destiny and the abominable indifference of nature.

Still it was not the man, but the horse, that suggested the tremendous question. One felt that somehow the man could change his station if he tried, but the horse was a servant of servants, under man and under nature. The broad, kindly, obedient face! It was enough to break a body's heart to sit still and look down into it. No trace of doubt or rebellion or complaint, only an appealing meekness as of one who tries to do as well as he can understand. Great simple-hearted slave! How will you answer when your master is judged by the King of Kings? How will he explain away his brutality to you when at last One shall say to him, "Why are these marks on the body of my servant?"

The Good Book tells us on many a page how, when we meet him, we shall know the righteous, but nowhere does it tell more clearly than where it says, he is merciful to his beast. In the Hills there was no surer way to find trouble than to strike the horse of the cattle-drover. I have seen an indolent blacksmith booted across his shop because he kicked a horse on the leg to make him hold his foot up. And I have seen a lout's head broken because the master caught him swearing at a horse.

As we rode, the day opened, and leaf and grass blade glistened with the melting frost. The partridge called to his mate across the fields. The ground squirrel, in his striped coat, hurried along the rail fence, bobbing in and out as though he were terribly late for some important engagement. The blackbirds in great flocks swung about above the corn fields, man[oe]uvring like an army, and now and then a crow shouted in his pirate tongue as he steered westward to a higher hill-top.

All the people of the earth were about their business on this October morning. Sometimes an urchin passed us on his way to the grist mill, astride a bag of corn, riding some ancient patriarchal horse which, out of a wisdom of years, refused to mend his gait for all the kicking of the urchin's naked heels. And we hailed him for a cavalier.

Sometimes a pair of oxen, one red, one white, clanked by, dragging, hooked in the yoke-ring, a log chain that made a jerky trail in the road, like the track of a broken-backed snake, and we spoke to the driver, inquiring which one was the saddle horse, and if the team worked single of a Sunday. And he answered with some laughing jeer that set us shaking in our saddles.

We had passed the flat lands, and were half way up Thornberg's Hill, a long gentle slope, covered with vines and underbrush and second-growth poplar saplings, when I heard a voice break out in a merry carol,—a voice free, careless, bubbling with the joy of golden youth, that went laughing down the hillside like the voice of the happiest bird that was ever born. It rang and echoed in the vibrant morning, and we laughed aloud as we caught the words of it:

> "Can she bake a cherry pie, Billy Boy, Billy Boy?
> Can she bake a cherry pie, charming Billy?
> She can bake a cherry pie quick as a cat can wink its eye,
> She's a young thing and can't leave her mother."

It required splendid audacity to fling such rippling nonsense at the feathered choirs in the sassafras thickets, but they were all listening with the decorous attitude of a conventional audience. I marked one dapper catbird, perched on a poplar limb, who cocked his head and heard the singer through, and then made that almost imperceptible gesture with which a great critic indicates his approval of a novice. "Not half bad," he seemed to say,—this blasé old habitué of the thicket music-halls. "I shouldn't wonder if something could be made of that voice if it were trained a trifle."

We broke into a trot and, rounding a corner of the wood, came upon the singer. She was a stripling of a girl in a butternut frock, standing bolt upright on a woman's saddle, tugging away at a tangle of vines, her mouth stained purple with the big fox-grapes, her round white arms bare to the elbows, and a pink calico sun-bonnet dangling on her shoulders, held only by the broad strings around her throat.

The horse under her was smoking wet to the fetlocks. This piping miss had been stretching his legs for him. It was Patsy, a madcap protegée of Cynthia Carper, the biggest tomboy that ever climbed a tree or ran a saddle-horse into "kingdom come." She slipped down into the saddle when she saw us, and flung her grapes away into the thicket. We stopped in the turnpike opposite to the cross road in which her horse was standing and hailed her with a laugh.

She looked us over with the dimples changing around her funny mouth. "You are a mean lot," she said, "to be laughing at a lady."

"We are not laughing at a lady," I answered; "we're laughing at the fun your horse has been having. He's tickled to death."

"Well," she said, looking down at the steaming horse, "I had to get here."

"You had to get here?" I echoed. "Goodness alive! Nobody but a girl would run a horse into the thumps to get anywhere."

"Stupid," she said, "I've just had to get here,—there, I didn't mean that. I meant I had to get where I was going."

"You were in a terrible hurry a moment ago," said I.

"The horse had to rest," she pouted.

"You might have thought of that," I said, "a little earlier in your seven miles' run." Then I laughed. The idea of resting the horse was so delicious that Ump and Jud laughed too.

The horse's knees were trembling and his sides puffing like a bellows. Here was Brown Rupert, the fastest horse in the Carper stable, a horse that Cynthia guarded as a man might guard the ball of his eye, run literally off his legs by this devil-may-care youngster. I would have wagered my saddle against a sheepskin that she had started Brown Rupert on the jump from the horse-block and held him to a gallop over every one of those seven blessed miles.

"Well," she said, "are you going to ride on? Or are you going to sit there like a lot of grinning hoodlums?"

Ump pulled off his hat and swept a laughable bow over his saddle horn. "Where are you goin', my pretty maid?" he chuckled.

She straightened in the saddle, then dropped him a courtesy as good as he had sent, and answered, "Fair sir, I ride 'cross country on my own business." And she gathered up the bridle in her supple little hand.

Jud laughed until the great thicket roared with the echo. Sir Questioner had caught it on the jaw.

"My dear Miss Touch-me-not," I put in, "let me give you a piece of advice. That horse is winded. If you start him on the gallop, you'll burst him."

She lifted her chin and looked me in the eye. "A thousand thank you's," she said, "and for advice to you, sir, don't believe anything you hear." Then she turned Brown Rupert and rode down the way she had come, sitting as straight in the saddle as an empress. For a moment the sunlight filtering through the poplar branches made queer mottled spots of gold on her curly head, then the trees closed in, and we lost her.

I doubled over the pommel of my saddle and laughed until my sides ached. Jud slapped his big hand on the leg of his breeches. "I hope I may die!" he ejaculated. It was his mightiest idiom. But the crooked Ump was as solemn as a lord. He sat looking down his nose.

I turned to him when I got a little breath in me. "Don't be glum," I said. "The little spitfire is an angel. You're not hurt."

The hunchback rubbed his chin. "Quiller," he said, "don't the Bible tell about a man that met an angel when he was a goin' somewhere?"

"Yes," I laughed.

"What was that man's name?" said he.

"Balaam," said I.

"Well," said he, "that man Balaam was the second ass that saw an angel, an' you're the third one."

# CHAPTER VII
# THE MASTER BUILDERS

The road running into the south lands crosses the Valley River at two places,—at the foot of Thornberg's Hill and twenty miles farther on at Horton's Ferry. At the first crossing, the river bed is piled with boulders, and the river boils through, running like a millrace, a swift, roaring water without a ford. At Horton's Ferry the river runs smooth and wide and deep, a shining sheet of clear water, making a mighty bend, still ford-less, but placid enough to be crossed by a ferry, running with a heavy current when swollen by the rains, except in the elbow of the bend where it swings into a tremendous eddy.

Over the river, where the road meets it first, is a huge wooden bridge with one span. It is giant work, the stone abutment built out a hundred feet on either side into the bed of the plunging water, neither rail nor wall flanking this stone causeway, but the bare unguarded width of the road-bed leading up into the bridge.

On the lips of the abutment, the builders set two stone blocks, smooth and wide, and cut places in them for the bridge timbers. It was a piece of excellent judgment, since the great stones could not be broken from the abutment, and they were mighty enough to bear the weight of a mountain. The bridge rests on three sills, each a log that, unhewn, must have taken a dozen oxen to drag it. I have often wondered at the magnitude of this labour; how these logs were thrown across the boiling water by any engines known to the early man. It was a work for Pharaoh. On these three giant sleepers the big floor was laid, the walls raised, and the whole roofed, so that it was a covered road over the Valley.

The shingle roof and the boarded sides protected the timber framework from the beating of the elements. Dry, save for the occasional splash of the hissing water far below, the great bones of this bridge hardened and lasted like sills of granite. The shingle roof curled, cracked, and dropped off into the water; the floor broke through, the sides rotted, and were all replaced again and again. But the powerful grandsires who had come down from the Hills to lay a floor over the Valley were not intending to do that work again, and went about their labour like the giants of old times.

Indeed, a legend runs that these sills were not laid by men at all, but by the Dwarfs. As evidence of this folklore tale, it is pointed out that these logs have the mark of a rough turtle burned on their under surface like the turtle cut on the great stones in the mountains. And men differ about what wood they are of, some declaring them to be oak and others sugar, and still others a strange wood of which the stumps only are now found in the Hills. It is true that no mark of axe can be found on them, but this is no great wonder since the bark was evidently removed by burning, an ancient method of preserving the wood from rot.

We swung down Thornberg's Hill in a long trot, and on to the bridge. The river was swollen, a whirling mass of yellow water that surged and pounded and howled under the timber floor as though the mad spirits of the river still resented the work of the Dwarfs. It was the Valley's business to divide the land, and it had done it well, leaving the sons of Eve to bite their fingers until, on a night, the crooked people came stumbling down to take a hand in the matter.

We clattered through, and down a long abutment. It almost made one dizzy to look over. A rail or a tree limb would ride down into this devil's maw, or a log would come swimming, its back bobbing in the muddy water, and then strike the smooth nose of a boulder and go to splinters.

Beyond the mad river the mild morning world was a land of lazy quiet. The sky was as blue as a woman's eye, and the sun rose clear in his flaming cart. Along the roadside the little purple flowers of autumn peeped about under the green briers. The fields were shaggy with ragweed and dead whitetop and yellow sedge. The walnut and the apple trees were bare, and the tall sycamore stood naked in its white skin. Sometimes a heron flapped across the land, taking a short cut to a lower water, or a woodpecker dived from the tall timber, or there boomed from the distant wooded hollow the drum of some pheasant lover, keeping a forgotten tryst.

It was now two hours of midday, and the October sun was warm. Tiny streaks of dampness were beginning to appear on the sleek necks of the Cardinal and El Mahdi, and the Bay Eagle was swinging her head, a clear sign that the good mare was not entirely comfortable.

I turned to Ump. "There's something wrong with that bridle," I said. "Either the brow-band or the throat-latch. The mare's fidgety."

He looked at me in astonishment, like a man charged suddenly with a crime, and slid his long hand out under her slim throat, and over her silk foretop; then he growled. "You don't know your A, B, C's, Quiller. She wants water; that's all."

Jud grinned like a bronzed Bacchus. "The queen might wear Spanish needles in her shirt," he said, "an' be damned. But the Bay Eagle will never wear a tight throat-latch or a pinchin' brow-band, or a rough bit, or a short headstall, while old Mr. Ump warms the saddle seat."

The hunchback was squirming around, craning his long neck. If the Bay Eagle were dry, water must be had, and no delay about it. Love for this mare was Ump's religion. I laughed and pointed down the road. "We are almost at Aunt Peggy's house. Don't stop to dig a well." And we broke into a gallop.

Aunt Peggy was one of the ancients, a carpet-weaver, pious as Martin Luther, but a trifle liberal with her idioms. The tongue in her head wagged like a bell-clapper. Whatever was whispered in the Hills got somehow into Aunt Peggy's ears, and once there it went to the world like the secret of Midas.

If one wished to publish a bit of gossip, he told Aunt Peggy, swore her to secrecy, and rode away. But as there is often a point of honour about the thief and a whim of the Puritan about the immoral, Aunt Peggy could never be brought to say who it was that told her. One could inquire as one pleased. The old woman ran no farther than "Them as knows." And there it ended and you might be damned.

The house was a log cottage covered with shingles and whitewash, set by the roadside under a great chestnut tree, its door always open in the daytime. As we drew rein by this open door, the old woman dropped her shuttle, tossed her ball of carpet rags over into the weaving frame, and came stumbling to the threshold in her long linsey dress that fell straight from her neck to the floor.

She pulled her square-rimmed spectacles down on her nose and squinted up at us. When she saw me, she started back and dropped her hands. "Great fathers!" she ejaculated, "I hope I may go to the blessed God if it ain't Quiller gaddin' over the country, an' Mister Ward a-dyin'."

It seemed to me that the earth lurched as it swung, and every joint in my body went limber as a rag. I caught at El Mahdi's mane, then I felt Jud's arm go round me, and heard Ump talking at my ear. But they were a long distance away. I heard instead the bees droning, and Ward's merry laugh, as he carried me on his shoulder a babbling youngster in a little white kilt. It was only an instant, but in it all the good days when I was little and Ward was father and mother and Providence, raced by.

Then I heard Ump. "It's a lie, Quiller, a damn lie. Don't you remember what Patsy said? Not to believe anything you hear? Do you think she ran that horse to death for nothin'? It was to tell you, to git to you first before

Woodford's lie got to you. Don't you see? Oh, damn Woodford! Don't you see the trick, boy?"

Then I saw. My heart gave a great thump. The sunlight poured in and I was back in the road by the old carpet-weaver's cottage.

The old woman was alarmed, but her curiosity held like a cable.

"What's he sayin'," she piped; "what's he sayin'?"

"That it's all a lie, Aunt Peggy," replied Jud.

She turned her squint eyes on him. "Who told you so?" she said.

"Who told you?" growled Ump.

"Them as knows," she said. And the curiosity piped in her voice. "Did they lie?"

"They did," said Ump; "Mister Ward's hurt, but he ain't dangerous."

"Bless my life," cried the old woman, "an' they lied, did they? I think a liar is the meanest thing the Saviour died for. They said Mister Ward was took sudden with blood poison last night, an' a-dyin', the scalawags! I'll dress 'em down when I git my eyes on 'em."

"Who were they, Aunt Peggy?" I ventured.

She made a funny gesture with her elbows, and then shook her finger at me. "You know I can't tell that, Quiller," she piped, "but the blessed God knows, an' I hope He'll tan their hides for 'em."

"I know, too," said Ump.

The old woman leaned out of the door. "Hey?" she said; "what's that? You know? Then maybe you'll tell why they come a-lyin'."

"Can you keep a secret?" said Ump, leaning down from his saddle.

The old woman's face lighted. She put her hand to her ear and craned her neck like a turtle. "Yes," she said, "I can that."

"So can I," said Ump.

The old carpet-weaver snorted. "Humph," she said, "when you git dry behind the ears you won't be so peart." Then she waved her hand to me. "Light off," she said, "an' rest your critters, an' git a tin of drinkin' water."

After this invitation she went back to her half-woven carpet with its green chain and its copperas-coloured widths, and we presently heard the hum of the wooden shuttle and the bang of the loom frame. We rode a few steps farther to the well, and Jud dismounted to draw the water. The appliance for lifting the bucket was of the most primitive type. A post with a forked top stood planted in the ground. In this fork rested a long, slender sapling with a heavy butt, and from the small end, high in the air, hung a slim pole, to the lower end of which the bucket was tied.

Jud grasped the pole and lowered the bucket into the well, and then, while one watched by the door, the others watered the horses in the old carpet-weaver's bucket. It was the only thing to drink from, and if Aunt Peggy had caught us with the "critters'" noses in it we should doubtless have come in for a large share of that "dressing down" which she was reserving for Lemuel Marks.

She came to the door as we were about to ride away and looked over the sweaty horses. "Sakes alive," she said, "you little whelps ride like Jehu. You'll git them horses ga'nted before you know it."

"You can't ga'nt a horse if he sweats good," said Ump; "but if he don't sweat, you can ga'nt him into fiddle strings."

"They're pretty critters," said the old woman, running her eyes over the three horses. "Be they Mister Ward's?"

"We all be Mister Ward's," answered Ump, screwing his mouth to one side and imitating the old carpet-weaver's voice.

"Bless my life," said the old woman, looking us up and down, "Mister Ward has a fine chance of scalawags."

We laughed and the old woman's face wrinkled into smiles. Then she turned to me. "Which way did you come, Quiller?" she asked.

"Over the bridge," said I. Now there was no other way to come, and the old carpet-weaver turned the counter with shrewd good-nature.

"Maybe you know how the bridge got there," she said.

"I've heard that the Dwarfs built it," said I, "but I reckon it's talk."

"Well, it ain't talk," said the old woman. "A long time ago, folks lived on the other side of the river, and the Dwarfs lived on this side, an' the folks tried to git acrost, but they couldn't, an' they talked to the Dwarfs over the river, an' asked them to build a bridge, an' the Dwarfs said they couldn't build it unless the river devils was bought off. Then the folks asked how to buy off them river devils, an' the Dwarfs said to throw in a thimble full of human blood an' spit in the river. So, one night the folks done it, an' next morning them logs was acrost."

The spectacles of the old woman were fastened around her head with a shoestring. She removed them by lifting the shoestring over her head, polished them for a moment on her linsey dress and set them back on her nose.

"Then," she went on, "the devilment was done. Just like it allers is when people gits smarter than the blessed God. The Dwarfs crost over an' rid the horses in the night an' sucked the cows, an' made faces at the women so the children was cross-eyed. An' the folks tried to throw down the bridge an' couldn't do it because the Dwarfs had put a spell on them logs."

She stopped and jerked her thumb toward the river. "Did you ever hear tell of old Jimmy Radcliff?" she asked.

We had heard of the old-time millwright, and said so.

"Well," she went on, "they was a-layin' a floor in that bridge oncet, an' old Jimmy got tight on b'iled cider, an' 'low'd he'd turn one of them logs over. So he chucked a crowbar under one of 'em an' begun a-pryin', an' all at oncet that crowbar flew out of his hand an' old Jimmy fell through, an' the men cotched him by his wampus an' it took four of 'em to pull him up, because, they said, it felt like somethin' was a-holdin' his legs."

"I reckon," said Ump, "it was the cider in Jimmy's legs. If there had been anything holdin', they could have seen it."

"'Tain't so certain," said Aunt Peggy, wagging her head, "'tain't so certain. There's many a thing a-holdin' in the world that you can't see." And she turned around in the door and went stumping back to her loom.

We rode south in no light-hearted mood. Again we had met the far-sighted cunning of Hawk Rufe, in a trap baited by a master, and had slipped from under it by no skill of ours. Had we missed those last words of Patsy, flung back like an angry taunt, I should have believed the tale about my brother and hurried north, if all the cattle in the Hills had gone to the devil. It was a master move, that lie, and I began to see the capacity of these dangerous men. This was merely an outpost strategy, laid as they passed along. What would it be when we came to the serious business of the struggle?

And how came that girl on Thornberg's Hill? Cynthia was shoulder to shoulder with Woodford. We had seen that with our own eyes. Had Patsy turned traitor to Cynthia?

I looked over at Ump. "What did that little girl mean?" I said.

"I give it up," said he.

"I don't understand women," said I.

"If you did," said he, "they'd have you in a side-show."

# CHAPTER VIII
# SOME REMARKS OF SAINT PAUL

A great student of men has written somewhere about the fear that hovers at the threshold of events. And a great essayist, in a dozen lines, as clean-cut as the work of a gem engraver, marks the idleness of that fear when above the trembling one are only the gods,—he alone, with them alone.

The first great man is seeing right, we know. The other may be also seeing right, but few of us are tall enough to see with him, though we stand a-tiptoe. We sleep when we have looked upon the face of the threatening, but we sleep not when it crouches in the closet of the to-morrow. Men run away before the battle opens, who would charge first under its booming, and men faint before the surgeon begins to cut, who never whimper after the knife has gone through the epidermis. It is the fear of the dark.

It sat with me on the crupper as we rode into Roy's tavern. Marks and Peppers and the club-footed Malan were all moving somewhere in our front. Hawk Rufe was not intending to watch six hundred black cattle filing into his pasture with thirty dollars lost on every one of their curly heads. Fortune had helped him hugely, or he had helped himself hugely, and this was all a part of the structure of his plan. Ward out of the way first! Accident it might have been, design I believed it was. Yet, upon my life, with my prejudice against him I could not say.

That we could not tell the whims of chance from the plans of Woodford was the best testimonial to this man's genius. One moved a master when he used the hands of Providence to lift his pieces. The accident to Ward was clear accident, to hear it told. At the lower falls of the Gauley, the road home runs close to the river and is rough and narrow. On the opposite side the deep laurel thickets reach from the hill-top to the water. Here, in the roar of the falls, the Black Abbot had fallen suddenly, throwing Ward down the embankment. It was a thing that might occur any day in the Hills. The Black Abbot was a bad horse, and the prediction was common that he would kill Ward some day. But there was something about this accident that was not clear. Mean as his fame put him, the Black Abbot had never been known to fall in all of his vicious life. On his right knee there was a great furrow, long as a man's finger and torn at one corner. It was scarcely the sort of wound that the edge of a stone would make on a falling horse.

Ump and Jud and old Jourdan examined this wound for half a night, and finally declared that the horse had been shot. They pointed out that this was the furrow of a bullet, because hair was carried into the wound, and nothing but a bullet carries the hair with it. The fibres of the torn muscle were all forced one way, a characteristic of the track of a bullet, and the edge of the wound on the inside of the horse's knee was torn. This was the point from which a bullet, if fired from the opposite side of the river, would emerge; and it is well known that a bullet tears as it comes out. At least this is always true with a muzzle-loading rifle. Ward expressed no opinion. He only drew down his dark eyebrows when the three experts went in to tell him, and directed them to swing Black Abbot in his stall, and bandage the knee. But I talked with Ump about it, and in the light of these after events it was tolerably clear.

At this point of the road, the roar of the falls would entirely drown the report of a rifle, and the face of any convenient rock would cover the flash. The graze of a bullet on the knee would cause any horse to fall, and if he fell here, the rider was almost certain to sustain some serious injury if he were not killed. True, it was a piece of good shooting at fifty yards, but both Peppers and Malan could "bark" a squirrel at that distance.

If this were the first move in Woodford's elaborate plan, then there was trouble ahead, and plenty of trouble. The horses came to a walk at a little stream below Roy's tavern, and we rode up slowly.

The tavern was a long, low house with a great porch, standing back in a well-sodded yard. We dismounted, tied the horses to the fence, and crossed the path to the house. As I approached, I heard a voice say, "If the other gives 'em up, old Nicholas won't." Then I lifted the latch and flung the door open.

I stopped with my foot on the threshold. At the table sat Lem Marks, his long, thin legs stretched out, and his hat over his eyes. On the other side was Malan and, sitting on the corner of the table, drinking cider from a stone pitcher, was Parson Peppers,—the full brood.

The Parson replaced the pitcher and wiped his dripping mouth on his sleeve. Then he burst out in a loud guffaw. "I quote Saint Paul," he cried. "Do thyself no harm, for we are all here."

Marks straightened in his chair like a cat, and the little eyes of Malan slipped around in his head. For a moment, I was undecided, but Ump pushed through and I followed him into the room.

There was surprise and annoyance in Marks's face for a moment. Then it vanished like a shadow and he smiled pleasantly. "You're late to dinner," he said; "perhaps you were not expected."

"I think," said I, "that we were not expected, but we have come."

"I see," said Marks.

Peppers broke into a hoarse laugh and clapped his hand on Marks's shoulder. "You see, do you?" he roared; "you see now, my laddie. Didn't I tell you that you couldn't stop runnin' water with talk?"

The suggestion was dangerously broad, and Marks turned it. "I recall," he said, "no conversation with you about running water. That cider must be up in your hair."

"Lemuel, my boy," said the jovial Peppers, "the Lord killed Ananias for lyin' an' you don't look strong."

"I'm strong enough to keep my mouth shut," snapped Marks.

"Fiddle-de-dee," said Peppers, "the Lord has sometimes opened an ass's mouth when He wanted to."

"He didn't have to open it in your case," said Marks.

"But He will have to shut it in my case," replied Peppers; "you're a little too light for the job."

The cider was reaching pretty well into the Reverend Peppers. This Marks saw, and he was too shrewd to risk a quarrel. He burst into a laugh. Peppers began to hammer the table with his stone pitcher and call for Roy.

The tavern-keeper came in a moment, a short little man with a weary smile. Peppers tossed him the pitcher. "Fill her up," he roared, "I follow the patriarch Noah. He was the only one of the whole shootin' match who stood in with the Lord, an' he got as drunk as a b'iled owl."

Then he turned to us. "Will you have a swig, boys?"

We declined, and he struck the table with his fist. "Ho! ho," he roared; "is every shingle on the meetin'-house dry?" Then he marked the hunchback sitting by the wall, and pointed his finger at him. "Come, there, you camel, wet your hump."

That a fight was on, I had not the slightest doubt in the world. I caught my breath in a gasp. I saw Jud loosen his arm in his coat-sleeve. Ump was as sensitive as any cripple, and he was afraid of no man. To my astonishment he smiled and waved his hand. "I'm cheek to your jowl, Parson," he said; "set out the O-be-joyful."

"Hey, Roy!" called Peppers, "bring another pitcher for Humpty Dumpty." Then he kicked the table with his great cowhide boots and began to bellow:

> "Zaccheus he clum a tree
> His Lord an' Master for to see;
> The limb did break an' he did fall,
> An' he didn't git to see his Lord at all."

Ump and I were seated by the wall, tilted back in the tavern-keeper's split-bottom chairs, while Jud leaned against the door.

The rhyme set the Parson's head to humming, and he began to pat his leg. Then he spied Jud. "Hey, there! Beelzebub," he roared, "can you dust the puncheons?"

"When the devil's a-fiddlin'," said Jud.

"Ho, the devil," hummed the Parson.

> "As I set fiddlin' on a tree
> The devil shot his gun at me.
> He missed my soul an' hit a limb,
> An' I don't give a damn for him."

He slapped his leg to emphasise the "damn." At this moment Roy came in with the two stone pitchers, handed one to Ump and put the other down by the boisterous Parson.

Peppers turned to him. "Got a fiddle?" he asked.

"I think there's an old stager about," said Roy.

"Bring her in," said Peppers. Then he seized the pitcher by its stone handle and raised it in the air. "Wine's a mocker," he began, "an' strong drink is ragin', but old Saint Paul said, 'A little for your stomach's sake.' Here's lookin' at you, Humpty Dumpty. May you grow until your ears drag the ground."

The hunchback lifted his pitcher. "Same to you, Parson," he said, "an' all your family." Then they thrust their noses into the stone pitchers. Peppers gulped a swallow, then he lowered his pitcher and looked at Ump.

"Humpty Dumpty," he said, speaking slowly and turning down his thumb as he spoke, "when you git your fall, it'll be another job for them king's horses."

"Parson," said Ump, "I know how to light."

"How?" said Peppers.

"Easy," said Ump.

Peppers roared. "You ain't learned it any too quick," he said. "What goes up, has got to come down, an' you're goin' up end over appetite."

"When do I hit the ground, Parson?" asked Ump, with his nose in the pitcher.

Peppers spread out two of his broad fingers. "To-day is to-day," he said, "an' to-morrow is to-morrow. Then—" But the cunning Marks was on his feet before the sentence was finished.

"Peppers," he snapped, "you clatter like a feed-cutter. What are you tryin' to say? Out with it. Let's hear it."

It was a bold effort to throw us off the scent. Peppers saw the lead, and for a moment he was sober.

"I was a-warnin' the lost sinner," he said, "like Jonah warned the sinners in Nineveh. I'm exhortin' him about the fall. Adam fell in the Garden of Eden." Then the leer came back into his face. "Ever hear of the Garden of Eden, Lemuel?"

"Yes," said Marks, glad to divert the dangerous drunkard.

"You ought," said Peppers. "Your grandpap was there, eatin' dirt an' crawlin' on his belly."

We roared, and while the tavern was still shaking with it, Roy came in carrying an old and badly battered fiddle under his arm. "Boys," he said timidly, "furse all you want to, but don't start nothin'." Then he gave the fiddle to Peppers, and came over to where we were seated. "Quiller," he said, "I reckon you all want a bite o' dinner."

I answered that we did. "Well," he apologised, "we didn't have your name in the pot, but we'll dish you up something, an' you can give it a lick an' a promise." Then he gathered up some empty dishes from a table and went out.

Peppers was thumping the fiddle strings with his thumb, and screwing up the keys. His sense of melody was in a mood to overlook many a defect, and he presently thrust the fiddle under his chin and began to saw it. Then he led off with a bellow,

"Come all ye merry maidens an' listen unto me."

But the old fiddle was unaccustomed to so vigorous a virtuoso, and its bridge fell with a bang. The Parson blurted an expletive, inflected like the profane. Then he straightened the bridge, gave the fiddle a tremendous saw, and resumed his bellow. But with the accident, his first tune had gone glimmering, and he dropped to another with the agility of an acrobat.

> "In eighteen hundred an' sixty-five
> I thought I was quite lucky to find myself alive.
> I saddled up old Bald Face my business to pursue,
> An' I went to drivin' steers as I used for to do."

The fiddle was wofully out of tune, and it rasped and screeched and limped like a spavined colt, but the voice of Peppers went ahead with the bellow.

> "But the stillhouse bein' close an' the licker bein' free
> I took to the licker, an' the licker took to me.
> I took to the licker, till I reeled an' I fell,
> An' the whole cussed drove went a-trailin' off to hell."

Ump arose and waved his pitcher. "Hold up, Parson," he said. "Here's to them merry maids that got lost in the shuffle. 'Tain't like you to lose 'em."

The suggestion was timely. The song ran to fifty-nine verses, and no others printable.

Peppers dropped the fiddle and seized the pitcher. "Correct," he roared. "Here's to 'em. May the Lord bless 'em, an' bind 'em, an' tie their hands behind 'em, an' put 'em in a place where the devil can't find 'em."

"Nor you," mumbled Ump in the echo.

They drank, and the hunchback eyed his man over the rim of the pitcher. The throat of the Parson did not move. It was clear that Peppers had reached the danger line, and, what was fatal to the plan of Ump, he knew it. He was shamming. The eyes of the hunchback squinted an instant, and then hardened in his face.

He lowered his pitcher, took a step nearer to the table, and clashed it against the Parson's pitcher. "The last one," he said, "to Mister Ward, God bless 'im!"

It was plain that the hunchback having failed to drink Peppers maudlin, was now deliberately provoking a fight. The bloated face of the Parson grew purple.

"Woodford!" he roared.

"I said," repeated Ump slowly, "to Mister Ward. An' his enemies, may the devil fly away with 'em."

Peppers hurled down his pitcher, and it broke into a thousand pieces on the oak floor. I saw the hunchback's eyes blink. I saw Jud take a step towards Peppers, but he was too late. Lem Marks made a sign to Malan. The club-footed giant bounded on Peppers, pinned his arms to his sides, and lifting him from the table carried him toward the door. A fight in Roy's tavern was not a part of the plan of Hawk Rufe.

For a moment the Parson's rage choked him, and he fought and sputtered. Then he began to curse with terrible roaring oaths that came boiling up, oaths that would have awakened new echoes in the foul hold of any pirate ship that ever ran.

His bloodshot eyes rolled and glared at the hunchback over the woolly head of Malan. There seemed to be something in Ump's face that lashed the drunkard to a fury. I looked at Ump to see what it was, and unless I see the devil, I shall never see the like of that expression. It was the face of a perfectly cool imp.

Black Malan carried Peppers through the door as though he were a bushel of corn in a bag, and I marked the build of this powerful man. His neck had muscle creases like the folds on the neck of a muley bull. His shoulders were bigger than Jud's. His arms were not so long, but they were thicker, and his legs stood under him like posts. But he was slow, and he had but little light in his head. A tremendous animal was the club-footed Malan.

Lem Marks stopped at the door, fingered his hat and began to apologise. He was sorry Peppers was drunk, and we must overlook the vapourings of a drunkard. He wished us a pleasant journey.

"To the devil," added Ump when the door had closed on him.

# CHAPTER IX
# CHRISTIAN THE BLACKSMITH

We ate our dinner from the quaint old Dutch blue bowls, and the teacups with the queer kneeling purple cows on them. Then we went to feed the horses. Roy brought us a hickory split basket filled with white corn on the cob, and wiped out a long chestnut trough which lay by the roadside. We took the bits out of the horses' mouths, leaving the headstalls on them, and they fell to with the hearty impatience of the very hungry.

I have always liked to see a horse or an ox eat his dinner. Somehow it makes the bread taste better in one's own mouth. They look so tremendously content, provokingly so I used to think when I was little, especially the ox with the yoke banging his horns. I remember how I used to fill my pockets with "nubbins" and, holding one out to old Berry or some other patriarch of the work cattle, watch how he reached for it with his rough tongue, and how surprised he was when I snatched it away and put it back in my pocket, or gave it to him, and then thrust my finger against his jaw, pushing in his cheek so that he could not eat it. He would look so wofully hurt that I laughed with glee until old Jourdan came along, gathered me up under his arm, and carried me off kicking to the kingdom of old Liza.

My early experience with the horse was not so entirely satisfactory to my youthful worship. Somewhere on my shoulder to this day are the faint marks of teeth, set there long ago on a winter morning when I was taking liberties with the table etiquette of old Charity.

We lolled in the sunshine while the horses ate, Jud on his back by the nose of the Cardinal, his fingers linked under his head. I sat on the poplar horse-block with my hands around my knee, while Ump was in the road examining El Mahdi's feet. For once he had abandoned the Bay Eagle.

He rubbed the fetlocks, felt around the top of the hoofs with his finger, scraped away the clinging dirt with the point of a knife blade, and tried the firmness of each shoe-nail. Then he lifted the horse's foot, rested it on his knee, and began to examine the shoe as an expert might examine some intricate device.

Ump held that bad shoeing was the root of all evil. "Along comes a flat-nose," he would say, "with a barefooted colt, an' a gabbin', chuckle-headed blacksmith nails shoes on its feet, an' the flat-nose jumps on an' away he goes, hipety click, an' the colt interferes, an' the flat-nose begins a kickin' an' a cursin', an' then—" Here the hunchback's fingers began to twitch. "Somebody ought to come along an' grab the fool by the scruff of his neck an' kick him till he couldn't set in a saddle, an' then go back an' boot the sole-leather off the blacksmith."

I have seen the hunchback stop a stranger in the road and point out with indignation that the shoe on his horse was too short, or binding the hoof, or too heavy or too light, and then berate the stranger like a thief because he would not turn instantly and ride back to a smith-shop. And I have seen him sit over a blacksmith with his narrow face thrust up under the horse's belly, and put his finger on the place where every nail was to go in and the place where it was to come out, and growl and curse and wrangle, until, if I had been that smith, I should have killed him with a hammer.

But the hunchback knew what he was about. Ward said of Ump that, in his field, the land of the horse's foot, he was as much an expert as any professor behind his spectacles. His knowledge came from the observation of a lifetime, gathered by tireless study of every detail. Even now, when I see a great chemist who knows all about some drug; a great surgeon who knows all about the body of a man; or a great oculist who knows all about the human eye, I must class the hunchback with them.

Ump explored El Mahdi's shoes, pulled at the calks, picked at the nails, and prodded into the frog of the foot to see if there was any tendency to gravel. He found a left hind shoe that did not suit him, and put down the foot and wiped his hands on his breeches.

"Who shod this horse, Quiller?" he said.

"Dunk Hodge," I answered.

The hunchback made a gesture as of one offered information that is patent. "I know Dunk made the shoes," he said, "by the round corks. But they've been reset. Who reset 'em?"

"Dunk," said I.

"Not by a jugful!" responded Ump. "Old Dunk never reset 'em."

"I sent the horse to him," I said.

"I don't care a fiddler's damn where you sent the horse," replied the hunchback. "Dunk didn't drive them nails. They're beat over at the point instead of being clinched. It's a slut job."

"I expect," said Jud, "it was his ganglin' son-in-law, Ab."

"That's the laddiebuck," said Ump, "an' he ought to be withed. That hind shoe has pulled loose an' broke. We've got to git it put on."

"Then we shall have to try Christian," said I; "there's no other shop this side of the Stone Coal."

"I know it," mused Ump, "an' when he goes to the devil, flat-nosed niggers will never shovel dirt on a meaner dog."

Jud arose and began to bridle the Cardinal. "He's mighty triflin'," said he; "he uses store nails, an' he's too lazy to p'int 'em."

Now, to use the manufactured nail was brand enough in the Hills. But to drive it into a horse's foot without first testing the point was a piece of turpitude approaching the criminal.

"Well," said I, "he'll drive no nail into El Mahdi that isn't home-made and smooth."

"Then Ump 'ill have to stand over him," replied Jud.

"Damn it," cried the hunchback, striking his clenched right hand into the palm of his left, "ain't I stood over every one of the shirkin' pot-wallopers from the mountains to the Gauley an' showed him how to shoe a horse, an' told him over an' over just what to do an' how to do it, an' put my finger on the place? An' by God! The minute my back's turned, he'll lame a horse with a splintered nail, or bruise a frog with a pinchin' cork, or pare off the toe of the best mare that ever walked because he's too damn' lazy to make the shoe long enough."

Ump turned savagely and went around El Mahdi to the Bay Eagle, put the bit in her mouth and mounted the mare. I bridled El Mahdi and climbed into the saddle, and we rode out toward the Valley River, on the way but an hour ago taken by the lieutenants of Woodford. We had watched them from the tavern door, Peppers riding between the other two, rolling in his saddle and brandishing his fist. Both he and Malan rode the big brown cattle-horses of Woodford, while Lem Marks rode a bay Hambletonian, slim and nervous, with speed in his legs. The saddles were all black, long skirted, with one girth,—the Woodford saddles.

We followed in the autumn midday. It might have been a scene from some old-time romance—musketeers of the King and guards of his mighty Eminence setting out on a mission which the one master wished and the other wished not; or the iron lieutenants of Cromwell riding south in the wake of the cavaliers of Charles.

For romance, my masters, is no blear-eyed spinster mooning over the trumpery of a heyday that is gone, but a Miss Mischief offering her dainty fingers to you before the kiss of your grandfather's lips is yet dry on them. The damask petticoat, the powdered wig, and the coquettish little patch by her dimpled little mouth are off and into the garret, and she sweeps by in a Worth gown, or takes a fence on a thoroughbred, or waits ankle deep in the clover blossoms for some whistling lover, while your eyes are yet a-blinking.

The blacksmith-shop sat at a crossroads under a fringe of hickory trees that skirted a little hill-top. It was scarcely more than a shed, with a chimney, stone to the roof, and then built of sticks and clay. Out of this chimney the sparks flew when the smith was working, pitting the black shingle roof and searing the drooping leaves of the hickories. Around the shop was the characteristic flotsam, a cart with a mashed wheel, a plough with a broken mould-board, innumerable rusted tires, worn wagon-irons, and the other wreckage of this pioneer outpost of the mechanic.

At the foot of the hill as we came up, the Cardinal caught a stone between the calks of one of his hind shoes, and Jud got off to pry it out. Ump and I rode on to the shop and dismounted at the door. Old Christian was working at the forge welding a cart-iron, pulling the pole of his bellows, and pausing now and then to turn the iron in the glowing coals.

He was a man of middle size, perhaps fifty, bald, and wearing an old leather skull-cap pitted with spark holes. His nose was crooked and his eyes were set in toward it, narrow and close together. He wore an ancient leather apron, burned here and there and dirty, and his arms were bare to the elbows.

I led El Mahdi into the shop, and Christian turned when he heard us enter. "Can you tack on a shoe?" said I.

The smith looked us over, took his glowing iron from the forge, struck it a blow or two on the anvil, and plunged it sizzling into the tub of water that stood beside him. Then he came over to the horse. "Fore or hind?" he asked.

"Left hind," I answered; "it's broken."

He went to the corner of the shop and came back with his kit,—a little narrow wooden box on legs, with two places, one for nails and one for the shoeing tools, and a wooden rod above for handle and shoe-rack. He set the box beside him, took up the horse's foot, wiped it on his apron, and tried the shoe with his fingers. Then he took a pair of pincers out of his box, and catching one half of the broken shoe, gave it a wrench.

I turned on him in astonishment. "Stop," I cried, "you will tear the hoof."

"It'll pull loose," he mumbled.

Ump was at the door, tying the Bay Eagle. He came in when he heard me. "Christian," he said, "cut them nails."

The blacksmith looked up at him. "Who's shoein' this horse?" he growled.

The eyes of the hunchback began to snap. "You're a-doin' it," he said, "an' I'm tellin' you how."

"If I'm a doin' it," growled the blacksmith, "suppose you go to hell." And he gave the shoe another wrench.

I was on him in a moment, and he threw me off so that I fell across the shop against a pile of horseshoes. The hunchback caught up a sledge that lay by the door and threw it. Old Christian was on one knee. He dodged under the horse and held up the kit to ward off the blow. The iron nose of the sledge struck the box and crushed it like a shell, and, passing on, bounded off the steel anvil with a bang.

The blacksmith sprang out as the horse jumped, seized the hammer and darted at Ump. I saw the hunchback look around for a weapon. There was none, but he never moved. The next moment his head would have burst like a cracked nut, but in that moment a shadow loomed in the shop door. There was a mad rush like the sudden swoop of some tremendous hawk. The blacksmith was swept off his feet, carried across the shop, and flattened against the chimney of his forge. I looked on, half dazed by the swiftness of the thing. I did not see that it was Jud until old Christian was gasping under the falling mortar of his chimney, his feet dangling and his sooty throat caught in the giant's fingers, that looked like squeezing iron bolts. The staring eyes of the old man were glassy, his face was beginning to get black, his mouth opened, and his extended bare arm holding the hammer began to come slowly down.

It rested a moment on the giant's shoulder, then it bent at the elbow, the fingers loosed, and the hammer fell. Old Christian will never be nearer to the pit of his imperial master until he stumbles over its rim.

The hunchback glided by me and clapped his hand on Jud's shoulder. "Drop him," he cried.

The blood of the giant was booming. The desperate savage, passed sleeping from his father and his father's father, had awaked, and awaked to kill. I could read the sinister intent in the crouch of his shoulders.

The hunchback shook him. "Jud," he shouted, "Jud, drop him."

The giant turned his head, blinked his eyes for a moment like a man coming out of a sleep, and loosed his hand. The blacksmith slipped to the floor, but he could not stand when he reached it. His knees gave way. He caught the side of the leather bellows, and stumbling around it, sat down on the anvil wheezing like a stallion with the heaves.

Ump stooped and picked up the hammer. Then he turned to the puffing giant. "Jud," he said, "you ain't got sense enough to pour rain-water out of a boot."

"Why?" said Jud.

"Why?" echoed the hunchback, "why? Suppose you had wrung the old blatherskite's neck. How do you reckon we'd get a shoe on this horse?"

# CHAPTER X
# ON THE CHOOSING OF ENEMIES

It has been suggested by the wise that perhaps every passing event leaves its picture on the nearest background, and may hereafter be reproduced by the ingenuity of man. If so, and if genius led us into this mighty gallery of the past, there is no one thing I would rather look at than the face of a youth who stood rubbing his elbows in the shop of old Christian, the blacksmith.

The slides of violent emotion, thrust in when unexpected, work such havoc in a child's face,—that window to the world which half our lives are spent in curtaining!

I wish to see the face of the lad only if the gods please. The canvas about it is all tolerably clear,—the smoke-painted shop, and the afternoon sun shining in to it through the window by the forge; and through the great cracks, vertical sheets of sunlight thrust, wherein the golden dust was dancing; the blacksmith panting on his anvil, his bare arms bowed, and his hands pressed against his body as though to help somehow to get the good air into his lungs, beads of perspiration creeping from under the leather cap and tracing white furrows down his sooty face; Jud leaning against the wall, and Ump squatting near El Mahdi. The horse was not frightened. He jumped to avoid the flying sledge. That was all. I cannot speak of the magnitude of his courage. I can only say that he had the sublime indifference of a Brahmin from the Ganges.

Presently the blacksmith had gotten the air in him, and he arose scowling, picked up his tongs, fished the cart-iron out of the water, thrust it into the coals and began to pump his bellows.

It was an invitation to depart and leave him to his own business. But it was not our intention to depart with a barefooted horse, even if the devil were the blacksmith.

"Christian," said Ump, "you're not through with this horse."

The blacksmith paid no attention. He pumped his bellows with his back toward us.

"Christian!" repeated the hunchback, and his voice was the ugliest thing I have ever heard. It was low and soft and went whistling through the shop. "Do you hear me, Christian?"

The smith turned like an animal that hears a hissing by his heels, threw the tongs on the floor, and glared at Ump. "I won't do it," he snarled.

"Easy, Christian," said the hunchback, with the same wheedling voice that came so strangely through his crooked mouth. "Think about it, man. The horse is barefoot. We should be much obliged to you."

I do not believe that this man was a coward. It was his boast that he could shoe anything that could walk into his shop, and he lived up to the boast. I give him that due, on my honour. Many a devil walked into that shop wearing the hoof and hide of a horse and came out with iron nailed on his feet; for example, horses like the Black Abbot that fought and screamed when we put a saddle on him first and rolled on the earth until he crushed the saddle-tree and the stirrups into splinters; and horses like El Mahdi that tried to kill the blacksmith as though he were an annoying fly. It was dangerous business, and I do not believe that old Christian was a coward.

But what show had he? An arm's length away was the powerful Jud whose hand had just now held the smith out over the corner of the world; and the hunchback squatted on the floor with the striking hammer in his long fingers, the red glint under his half-closed eyelids, and that dangerous purring speech in his mouth. What show had he?

The man looked up at the roof, blackened with the smoke of half a century, and then down at the floor, and the resolution died in his face. He gathered up his scattered tools and went over to the horse, lifted his foot, cut the nails, and removed the pieces of broken shoe.

Then he climbed on the anvil, and began to move the manufactured shoes that were set in rows along the rafters, looking for a size that would fit.

"Them won't do," said Ump. "You'll have to make a shoe, Christian."

The man got down without a word, seized a bar of iron and thrust it into the coals. Jud caught the pole of his bellows, and pumped it for him. The smith turned the iron in the coals. When it glowed he took it out, cut off the glowing piece on the chisel in his anvil, caught it up in a pair of tongs and thrust it back into the fire. Then he waited with his hands hanging idly while Jud pulled the pole of the old bellows until it creaked and groaned and the fire spouted sparks.

When the iron was growing fluffy white, the smith caught it up in his tongs, lifted it from the fire, flung off a shower of hissing sparks and began to hammer, drawing it out and beating it around the horn of the anvil until presently it became a rough flat shoe.

The iron was cooling, and he put it back into the coals. When it was hot again, he turned the calks, punched the nail holes and carried it glowing to where the horse stood, held it an instant to the hoof, noted the changes to be made, and thrust it back into the fire.

A moment later the hissing shoe was plunged into a tub of water by the anvil, and then thrown steaming to the floor. Ump picked it up, passed his finger over it and then set it against El Mahdi's foot. It was a trifle narrow at the heel, and Ump pitched it back to the smith, spreading his fingers to indicate the defect. Old Christian sprung the calks on the horn of the anvil, and returned the shoe. The hunchback thrust his hand between the calks, raised the shoe and squinted along its surface to see if it were entirely level. Then he nodded his head.

The blacksmith went over to the wall, and began to take down a paper box. The hunchback saw him and turned under the horse. "We can't risk a store nail," he said. "You'll have to make 'em."

For the first time the man spoke. "No iron," he answered.

Ump arose and began to look over the shop. Presently he found an old scythe blade and threw it to the smith. "That'll do," he said; "take the back."

Old Christian broke the strip of iron from the scythe blade and heating it in his forge, made the nails, hammering them into shape, and cutting them from the rod until he had a dozen lying by the anvil. When they were cool, he gathered them in his hand, smoothed the points, and went over to El Mahdi.

The old man lifted the horse's foot, and set it on his knee, and Ump arose and stood over him. Then he shod the horse as the hunchback directed, paring the hoof and setting the nails evenly through the outer rim, clipping the nail ends, and clinching them by doubling the cut points. Then he smoothed the hoof with his great file and the work was over.

We rode south along the ridge, leaving old Christian standing in his shop door, his face sullen and his grimy arms folded. I flung him a silver dollar, four times the price of the shoeing. It fell by the shop sill, and he lifted his foot and sent it spinning across the road into the bushes.

The road ran along the ridge. A crumbling rail fence laced with the vines of the poison ivy trailed beside it. In its corners stood the great mullein, and the dock, and the dead iron-weed. The hickories, trembling in their yellow leaves, loomed above the fringe of sugar saplings like some ancient crones in petticoats of scarlet. Sometimes a partridge ran for a moment through the dead leaves, and then whizzed away to some deeper tangle in the woods; now a grey squirrel climbed a shell-bark with the clatter of a carpenter shingling a roof, and sat by his door to see who rode by, or shouted his jeer, and, diving into his house, thrust his face out at the window. Sometimes, far beyond us, a pheasant walked across the road, strutting as straight as a harnessed brigadier,—an outlaw of the Hills who had sworn by the feathers on his legs that he would eat no bread of man, and kept the oath. Splendid freeman, swaggering like a brigand across the war-paths of the conqueror!

We were almost at the crown of the ridge when a brown flying-squirrel, routed from his cave in a dead limb by the hammering of a hungry woodpecker, stood for a moment blinking in the sunlight and then made a flying leap for an oak on the opposite side of the road; but his estimate was calculated on the moonlight basis, and he missed by a fraction of an inch and went tumbling head over heels into the weeds.

I turned to laugh at the disconcerted acrobat, when I caught through the leaves the glimpse of a horse approaching the blacksmith-shop from one of the crossroads. I called to my companions and we found a break in the woods where the view was clear. At half a mile in the transparent afternoon we easily recognised Lem Marks. He rode down to the shop and stopped by the door.

In a moment old Christian came out, stood by the shoulder of the horse and rested his hand on Marks' knee. It was strange familiarity for such an acrimonious old recluse, and even at the distance the attitude of Woodford's henchman seemed to indicate surprise.

They talked together for some little while, then old Christian waved his arm toward the direction we had taken and went into his shop, presently returning with some implements in his hand. We could not make out what they were. He handed them up to Marks, and the two seemed to discuss the matter, for after a time Marks selected one and held it out to old Christian. The smith took it, turned it over in his hand, nodded his head and went back into his shop, while Marks gathered up his reins and came after us in a slow fox trot.

We slipped over the ridge and then straightened in our saddles.

"Boys," said the hunchback, fingering the mane of the Bay Eagle, "that was a bad job. We ought to be a little more careful in the pickin' of enemies."

"Damn 'em," muttered Jud, "I wonder what mare's nest they're fixin'. I ought to 'a twisted the old buck's neck."

The hunchback leaned over his saddle and ran his fingers along the neck of the splendid mare. "Peace," he soliloquised, "is a purty thing." Then he turned to me with a bantering, quizzical light in his eyes.

"Quiller," he said, "don't you wish you had your dollar back in your pocket?"

"Why?" said I.

"It's like this," said he. "One time there was an' old miser, an' when he was a-dyin' the devil come, an' set down by the bed, an' the devil said, 'You've done a good deal of work for me, an' I reckon I ought to give you a lift if you need it. Now, then, if there's any little thing you want done, I'll look after it for you.' The miser said he'd like to have an iron fence round his grave, if the devil thought he could see to it without puttin' himself out any. The devil said it wouldn't be any trouble, an' then he counted off on his fingers the minutes the miser had to live, an' lit out.

"They buried the miser in a poor corner of the graveyard where there was nothin' but sinkfield an' sand briars, an' that night the devil went down to the blacksmith an' told him he wanted an iron fence put around the old feller's grave, an' to git it done before midnight. The blacksmith throwed his coat an' went to work like a whitehead, an' when twelve o'clock come he had the iron fence done an' a settin' around the miser's grave.

"Just as the clock struck, the devil come along, an' he said to the blacksmith, standin' there a-sweatin' like a colt, 'Well, I see you got her all up hunkey dorey.' 'Yes,' said the blacksmith, 'an' now I want my pay.' 'Let's see about that,' said the devil; 'did you do that job because you wanted to, or because you didn't want to?' The blacksmith didn't know what to say, so he hemmed and hawed, an' finally he says, 'Maybe I done it because I wanted to, an' maybe I done it because I didn't want to.' 'All right,' said the devil; 'if you done it because you wanted to, I don't owe you nothin', an' if you done it because you didn't want to, there ain't nothin' I can pay you.' An' he sunk in the ground, with his thumb to his nose an' his fingers a-wigglin' at the blacksmith."

I saw the application of the story. One could settle with money for labour when the labourer was free, but when the labourer was not free, when he had used his breath and his muscle under a master, money could make no final settlement.

Ugly accounts to run in a world where the scheme of things is eternally fair, and worse, maybe, if carried over for adjustment into the Court of Final Equity! The remark of Ump came back like a line of ancient wisdom, "Peace is a purty thing."

# CHAPTER XI
# THE WARDENS OF THE RIVER

While men are going about with a bit of lens and a measure of acid, explaining the hidden things of this world, I should be very glad if they would explain why it is that the evening of an autumn day always recalls the lost Kingdom of the Little. The sun squinting behind the mountains, the blue haze deepening in the hollows of the hills, the cool air laden with faint odours from the nooks and corners of the world,—what have these to do with the land of the work-a-day?

Long and long ago in that other country it meant that the fairies were gathering under the hill for another raid on the province of the goblins across the sedge-fields; that the owls were going up on the ridges to whisper with the moon; that the elves one by one, in their quaint yellow coats, were stealing along under the oak trees on the trail of the wolf spider. But what can it mean in the grown-up country?

When the Golden Land is lost to us, when turning suddenly we find the enchanted kingdom vanished, do we give up the hope of finding it again? We know that it is somewhere across the world, and we ought to find it, and we know, too, that its out-country is like these October afternoons, and our hearts beat wildly for a moment, then the truth strikes and we see that this is not The Land.

But it brings the memory of the heyday of that other land, where, in my babyhood, like the kings of Bagdad, I had a hundred bay horses in their stables, each bridled with a coloured woollen string, and stalled in the palings of the garden, and each with his high-sounding name, and princely lineage, and his thrilling history, and where I had a thousand black cattle at pasture in the old orchard.

It might be that an ancient, passing, would not see the drove, because his eyes were hide-bound, but he would see me as I galloped along by the hot steers, and hear the shouting, and he could not doubt that they were there. I was tremendously busy in those earlier days. No cattle king of the Hills had one-half the wonderful business. I dropped to sleep in old Liza's arms with my mighty plans swimming in my head. I had long rides and many bunches of cattle to gather on to-morrow, and I must have a good night's rest.

Or I rode in Ward's arms, when he went to salt the cattle, and sat in the saddle while he threw the handfuls of salt on the weeds, and I noticed all the wonders of the land into which we came. I saw the golden-belted bee booming past on his mysterious voyage, and he was a pirate sailing the summer seas. I heard the buzzing curse of the bald hornet, and I wished him hard luck on his robbing raid. And the swarms of yellow butterflies were bands of stranger fairies travelling incognito. I knew what these fellows were about, but I said nothing. The ancients were good enough folk, but their idea of perspective was abominably warped. I gave them up pretty early.

The hills by the great Valley River are a quiet country, sodded deep, with here and there an open grove like those in which the dreamers wandered with a garland of meadowsweet, or the fauns piped when the world was young. Through them, now and then, a little stream goes laughing, fringed with bulrushes and beds of calamus and fragrant mint, a narrow stream that runs chuckling through the stiff sod and spreads dimpling over the road on a bed of white sand, for all the world like a dodging sprite of the wood who laughs suddenly in some sunlit corner.

We splashed through one of these little brooks as the sun was setting, and El Mahdi's feet sank in the white sand. I watched the crystal water go bubbling over his hoofs and then pour with a gush into the shoe tracks which held the print like a mould. We left a silver trail or, now when the sun was slanting, a golden trail, big with the air of enchanted ventures.

When we came on the brow of the hills flanking the approaches to the Valley River it was already night. The outlines of the far-off mountains were blending into one huge shadow. It was now the wall of the world, with no path for a human foot. The hills were a purple haze, the trees along their crests making fantastic pictures against the sky. Beyond the land of living men, it seemed, an owl hooted, and a belated dove called and called like a moaning spirit wandering in some lost tarn of the Styx.

We rode down to the bend of the Valley River over a stretch of sandy land pre-empted by the cinque-foil and the running brier, the country of the woodcock and the eccentric kildee. We could hear the low, sullen roar of the river sweeping north around this big bend, long before we came to it. Under the stars there is no greater voice of power. We rode side by side in the deepening twilight, making huge shadows on the crunching sand. Up to this hour it seemed to me that we had been idling through some long and pleasant ride, with the loom of evil afar off in the front. We had talked of peril merrily together, as men loitering in a tavern talk easily of the wars. But now in the night, under the spell of the booming water, the atmosphere of responsibility returned.

Ward was depending upon me and the two beside me. Woodford's men moved back yonder in the Hills, and maybe they moved out there beyond the water, and we could see nothing and hear nothing but the sand grinding under the iron of a horse's shoe. In the night the face of the Valley River was not a pleasant thing to see. It ran muddy and swift, even with its banks, a bed of water a quarter of a mile in width, its yellow surface gleaming now and then in the dim light of the evening like the belly of some great snake.

Standing on its bank we could see the other shore, a line of grey fog. The yellow tongues of the water lapped the bank, and crept muttering in among the willows, an ominous, hungry brood.

The roar of the river, now that one stood beside it, seemed not so great. It was dull, heavy, low pitched, as though the vast water growled comfortably. The rains in the mountains had filled the bed brimming like a cup, even in the drought of summer. The valley was wide and deep in this bend,—too wide and too deep to be crossed by the ordinary bridge,—so the early men had set up a sort of ferry when they first came to this water.

It was a rude makeshift, the old men said, two dugouts of poplar lashed together and paddled, a thing that would carry a man and his horse, or perhaps a yoke of oxen. Now, the ferry was more pretentious. A wire cable stretched across the river, fastened on the south bank to a post set deep in the earth, and flanked by an abutment of sandstone, and on the north bank wound round a huge elm that stood by the road within a dozen yards of the river.

On this cable the boat ran, fastened with wire ropes and two pulleys, a sort of long, flat barge that would carry thirty cattle. The spanning cable made a great curve down the river, so that the strength of the current was almost sufficient to force the barge across, striking it obliquely against the dip of the wire. How the current could be made to do this work was to me one of the mysteries, but it did do it, guided and helped by the ferrymen. I have wondered at it a hundred times as I sat under El Mahdi's nose with my feet dangling over the side of the boat.

We stopped on the slope where the boat landed.

Jud threw back his shoulders and shouted; and someone answered from the other side, "Who-ee!" a call that is said to reach farther than any other human sound. It came high up over the water, clear enough, but as from a great distance. There were no bells at the crossings in this land. Every man carried a voice in his throat that could reach half a mile to the grazing steers on the sodded knobs.

The two sons of old Jonas Horton maintained the ferry as their father had done before them. It was an inheritance, and it was something more than this. It was a trust, a family distinction, like a title,—something which they were born into, as a Hindoo is born into his father's trade. If they had been ousted from this ferry, they would have felt themselves as hopelessly wronged as the descendants of an old house driven from their baronial estate.

The two, Mart and Danel, lived with the mother, a flat, withered old woman, in a log house by the river. They were tall, raw-boned, serious men, rarely leaving the river, and at such times hurrying back uneasy. Their faces at the church or in the village were anxious, as of one who leaves his house closed with a fire roaring in the chimney; or better, perhaps, of some fearful child who has stolen away from his daily everlasting task. Sometimes the mother would say, "There is no meal in the barrel," or, "You're drinking the last of the coffee;" and they would look at each other across the table, troubled, as men dire beset called upon to decrease the forces of a garrison. Then one would set out with a bag on his shoulder, throwing his long body forward at each step and dangling his arms, hurrying as though he ought not to take the time.

Presently the boat crept towards us out of the water, swung down swiftly and ground its nose in the bank. The two ferrymen were bareheaded, in their brown homespun coats. They had possibly been at supper, and turned around on their bench to answer through the open door. They inquired if we all wished to be set over, and we rode on to the boat for answer. The man in the bow reached up and caught the cable with a sort of iron wrench, and began to pull. The other took a pole lying by the horses' feet, thrust it against the bank and forced the boat out into the water. Then he also took a wrench from his pocket, and when his brother, walking down the length of the barge from bow to stern, reached the end, he caught the cable and followed, so that the pull on the wire was practically continuous.

The warm south wind blew stiffly in our faces and the horses shifted their feet uneasily. If the Valley River was ugly from its bank it was uglier from its middle. It tugged at the boat as though with a thousand clinging fingers, and growled and sputtered, and then seemed to quit it for a moment and whisper around the oak boards like invisible conspirators taking counsel in a closet. A scholar on that water nursing his sallow face in the trough of his hand would have fallen a-brooding on the grim boatman crossing to the shore that none may leave, or the old woman of the Sanza, poling her ghostly, everlasting raft; and had he listened, he could have heard the baying of the three-mouthed hound arousing the wardens of the Vedic Underworld to their infernal watching by that water we all must cross.

I think the hunchback had no idea of the moods of nature; at any rate they never seemed to affect him. To him all water was something to drink or something to swim in, and the earth was good pasture or hard road to ride a horse over. The grasp of no agnostic was more cynical. He inquired if any of Woodford's men had crossed that day, and was answered that they had not.

Then he began to hum a hoary roundelay about the splendid audacity of old Mister Haystack and his questionable adventures, set to an unprintable refrain of "Winktum bolly mitch-a-kimo," or some such jumble of words. I have never heard this song in the mouth of any other man. He must have found it somewhere among the dusty trumpery of forgotten old folk-lyrics, and when he sang it one caught the force of the Hebraic simile about the crackling of thorns under a pot.

Jud laughed, and the hunchback piped a higher cackle and dangled his bridle rein. "Humph," he said, "maybe you don't like that song."

"It ain't the song," replied Jud.

"Maybe you don't like the way I sing it," said he.

"It might be different," said Jud.

"Well," said he, "it wouldn't mean different."

Here I took a hand in the dialogue. "What does it mean anyhow?" I said. "It's about the foolest song I ever heard."

"Quiller," replied the hunchback, propping his fist under his bony jaw, "you've heard tell of whistlin' to keep up your courage. Well, that song was made for them as can't whistle."

Jud turned in astonishment. "Afraid?" he said; "what are you afraid of?"

The hunchback leaned over as if about to impart a secret. "Ghosts!" he whispered. I laughed at the discomfiture of the giant, but Ump went on counterfeiting a deep and weird seriousness which, next to his singing, was about the most ludicrous thing in the world. "Ghosts, my laddiebuck. But not the white-sheeted lady that comes an' says, 'Foller me,' nor the spook that carries his head under his arm tied up in a tablecloth, but ghosts, my laddiebuck, that make tracks while they walk."

"I thought ghosts rode broomsticks," said Jud.

"Nary a broomstick," replied the hunchback. "When they are a-follerin' Mister Ward's drovers, it's a little too peaked for long ridin'."

Then he broke off suddenly and called to the ferryman. "Danel," he said, "how many cattle will this boat hold?"

"Big cattle or stockers?" inquired the man.

"Exporters," said Ump.

"Mart," called the brother, "can we carry thirty exporters?"

"Are they dehorned?" inquired Mart.

"Muley," said Ump.

"We can carry thirty muleys if they ain't nervous," replied the brother called Mart. "Are you gatherin' up some cattle for Mister Ward?"

"Yes," said Ump. "We'll be here early in the morning with six hundred, an' we want to git 'em set over as quick as you can. How long will it take?"

"Well," said Danel, "mighty nigh up till noon, I reckon. Do you mind, Mart, how long we were settin' over them Alkire cattle?"

"We begun in the morning, and we stopp'd for an afternoon bite. It took the butt end of the day," replied the brother.

We had now reached the south bank of the Valley River, and when the boat slipped up on the wet sod, we rode ashore, and turned into the pike that runs by the river bank. The ferrymen, with the characteristic hospitality of the Hills, requested us to dismount and share the evening meal, but we declined, urging the lateness of the hour.

Through the open door I could see the unfinished supper, the sweet corn-pone cut like a great cheese, the striped bacon, and the blue stone milk pitcher with its broken ears.

# CHAPTER XII
# THE USES OF THE MOON

When I turned about in the saddle I found that El Mahdi had passed both of my companions who were stock still in the road a half-dozen paces behind me. I pulled him up and called to them, "What mare's nest have you found now?"

They replied that some horse had lately passed in a gallop. One could tell by the long jumping and the deep, ploughing hoof-prints. "Come on," said I, "Woodford's devils haven't crossed. What do we care?"

"But it's mighty big jumpin'," answered the hunchback.

"Maybe," I responded laughing, "the cow that jumped over the moon took a running start there."

"If she did," said Ump, "I'll just find out if any of the Hortons saw her goin'." Then he shouted, "Hey, Danel, who crossed ahead of us?"

The long bulk of the ferryman loomed in the door. "It was Twiggs," he answered.

I heard Jud cursing under his breath. Twiggs was the head groom of Cynthia Carper, and when he ran a horse like that the devil was to pay. I gripped the reins of El Mahdi's bridle until he began to rear.

"He must have been in a hurry," said Ump.

"'Pears like it," responded the boatman, turning back into his house. "He lit out pretty brisk."

Ump shook the reins of his bridle and went by me in a gallop. The Cardinal passed at my knee, and I followed, bending over to keep the flying sand out of my eyes.

The moon was rising, a red wheel behind the shifting fog. And under its soft light the world was a ghost land. We rode like phantoms, the horses' feet striking noiselessly in the deep sand, except where we threw the dead sycamore leaves. My body swung with the motions of the horse, and Ump and Jud might have been a part of the thing that galloped under their saddles.

The art of riding a horse cannot be learned in half a dozen lessons in the academy on the avenue. It does not lie in the crook of the knee, or the angle of the spine. It does not lie in the make of the saddle or the multiplicity of snaffle reins, nor does it lie in the thirty-nine articles of my lady's riding-master. But it is embraced in the grasp of one law that may be stated in a line, and perhaps learned in a dozen years,—be a part of the horse.

The mastery of an art—be it what you like—does but consist in the comprehension of its basic law. The appreciation of this truth is indispensable. It cannot avail to ape the manner of the initiate. I have seen dapper youths booted and spurred, riding horses in the park, rising to the trot and holding the ball of the foot just so on the iron of the stirrup, and if the horse had bent his body they would have gone sprawling into the bramble bushes. Yet these youngsters believed that they were riding like her Majesty's cavalry, the ogled gallants of every strolling lass.

I have seen begloved clubmen with an English accent worrying a good horse that they understood about as well as a problem in mechanics or any line of Horace. And I have seen my lady sitting a splendid mount, with the reins caught properly in her fingers and her back as straight as a whip-staff, and I would have wagered my life that every muscle in her little body was as rigid as a rock, and her knee as numb as the conscience of a therapeutist.

Look, if you please, at the mud-stained cavalryman who has lived his days and his nights in the saddle; or the cattle drover who has never had any home but this pigskin seat, and mark you what a part of the horse he is. Hark back to these models when you are listening to the vapourings of a riding-master lately expatriated from the stables of Sir Henry. To ride well is to recreate the fabulous centaur of Thessaly.

We raced over the mile of sand road in fewer minutes than it takes to write it down here. There was another factor, new come into the problem, and we meant to follow it close. Expedition has not been too highly sung. An esoteric novelist hath it that a pigmy is as good as a giant if he arrive in time.

At the end of this mile, below Horton's Ferry, the road forks, and there stands a white signboard with its arms crossed, proclaiming the ways to the travelling stranger. The cattle Ward had bought were in two droves. Four hundred were on the lands of Nicholas Marsh, perhaps three miles farther down the Valley River, and the remaining two hundred a mile or two south of the crossroads at David Westfall's.

Ump swung his horse around in the road at the forks. "Boys," he said, "we'll have to divide up. I'll go over to old Westfall's, an' you bring up the other cattle. I'll make King David help to the forks."

"What about Twiggs?" said I.

"To hell with Twiggs," said he. "If he gits in your way, throat him." Then he clucked to the Bay Eagle and rode over the hill, his humped back rising and falling with the gallop of the mare.

We slapped the reins on our horses' necks and passed on to the north, the horses nose to nose, and my stirrup leather brushing the giant's knee at every jump of El Mahdi. The huge Cardinal galloped in the moonlight like some splendid machine of bronze, never a misstep, never a false estimate, never the difference of a finger's length in the long, even jumps. It might have been the one-eyed Agib riding his mighty horse of brass, except that no son of a decadent Sultan ever carried the bulk of Orange Jud. And the eccentric El Mahdi! There was no cause for fault-finding on this night. He galloped low and easily, gathering his grey legs as gracefully as his splendid, nervous mother. I watched his mane fluttering in the stiff breeze, his slim ears thrust forward, the moon shining on his steel-blue hide. For once he seemed in sympathy with what I was about. Seemed, I write it, for it must have been a mistaken fancy. This splendid, indifferent rascal shared the sensations of no living man. Long and long ago he had sounded life and found it hollow. Still, as if he were a woman, I loved him for this accursed indifference. Was it because his emotions were so hopelessly inaccessible, or because he saw through the illusion we were chasing; or because—because—who knows what it was? We have no litmus-paper test for the charm of genius.

Under us the dry leaves crackled like twigs snapping in a fire, and the flying sand cut the bushes along the roadway like a storm of whizzing hailstones. In the wide water of the Valley River the moon flitted, and we led her a lively race. When I was little I had a theory about this moon. The old folks were all wrong about its uses. Lighting the night was a piece of incidental business. It was there primarily as a door into and out of the world. Through it we came, carried down from the hill-tops on the backs of the crooked men and handed over to the old black mammy who unwrapped us trembling by the firelight. Then we squalled lustily, and they said "A child is born."

When a man died, as we have a way of saying, he did but go back with these same crooked men through the golden door of the world. Had I not seen the moon standing with its rim on the eastern ridge of the Seely Hill when they found old Jerry Lance lying stone-dead in his house? And had I not predicted with an air of mysterious knowledge that Jourdan would recover when Red Mike threw him? The sky was moonless and he could not get out if he wished.

Besides there was a lot of mystery about this getting into the world. Often when I was little, I had questioned the elders closely about it, and their replies were vague, clothed in subtle and bedizzened generalities. They did not know, that was clear, and since they were so abominably evasive I was resolved to keep the truth locked in my own bosom and let them find out about it the best way they could. Once, in a burst of confidence I broached the subject to old Liza and explained my theory. She listened with a grave face and said that I had doubtless discovered the real truth of the matter, and I ought to explain it to a waiting world. But I took a different view, swore her to secrecy, and rode away on a peeled gum-stick horse named Alhambra, the Son of the Wind.

While the horses ran, I speculated on the possible mission of Twiggs, but I could find no light, except that, of course, it augured no good to us. I think Jud was turning the same problem, for once in a while I could hear him curse, and the name of Twiggs flitted among the anathemas. We had hoped for a truce of trouble until we came up to Woodford beyond the Valley River. But here was a minion of Cynthia riding the country like Paul Revere. My mind ran back to the saucy miss on the ridge of Thornberg's Hill, and her enigmatic advice, blurted out in a moment of pique. This Twiggs was colder baggage. But, Lord love me! how they both ran their horses!

Three miles soon slip under a horse's foot, and almost before we knew it we were travelling up to Nicholas Marsh's gate. Jud lifted the wooden latch and we rode down to the house. Ward said that Nicholas Marsh was the straightest man in all the cattle business, scrupulously clean in every detail of his trades. Many a year Ward bought his cattle without looking at a bullock of them. If Marsh said "Good tops and middlin' tails," the good ones of his drove were always first class and the bad ones rather above the ordinary. The name of Marsh was good in the Hills, and his word was good. I doubt me if a man can leave behind him a better fame than that.

The big house sat on a little knoll among the maples, overlooking the Valley River. The house was of grey stone, built by his father, and stood surrounded by a porch, swept by the maple branches and littered with saddles, saddle blankets, long rope halters, bridles, salt sacks, heavy leather hobbles, and all the work-a-day gear of a cattle grazier.

There was a certain air of strangeness in the way we were met at Nicholas Marsh's house. I do not mean inhospitality, rather the reverse, with a tinge of embarrassment, as of one entertaining the awkward guest. We were evidently expected, and a steaming supper was laid for us. Yet, when I sat at the table and Jud with his plate by the smouldering fire, we were not entirely easy. Marsh walked through the room, backward and forward, with his hands behind him, and a great lock of his iron-grey hair throwing shadows across his face. Now and then he put some query about the grass, or my brother's injury, or the condition of the road, and then turned about on his heel. His fine open face wore traces of annoyance. It was plain that there had been here some business not very pleasing to this honourable man. When I told him we had come for the cattle, the muscles of his jaw seemed to tighten. He stopped and looked me squarely in the face.

"Well, Quiller," he said, with what seemed to me to be unnecessary firmness, "I shall let you have them."

I heard Jud turn sharply in his chair.

"Let me have them? Is there any trouble about it?"

The man was clearly embarrassed. He bit his lip and twisted his neck around in his collar. "No," he said, hesitating in his speech, "there isn't any trouble. Still a man might demand the money at the scales. He would have a right to do that."

My pulse jumped. So this was one of their plans, those devils. And we had never a one of us dreamed of it. If the money were demanded at the scales it would mean delay, and delay meant that Woodford would win.

So this was Twiggs's part in the ugly work. No wonder he ran his horse. Trust a woman for jamming through the devil's business. Nothing but the good fibre of this honourable man had saved us. But Westfall! He was lighter stuff. How about Westfall?

I looked up sharply into the troubled face of the honest man.

"How about the other cattle," I faltered; "shall we get them?"

"Who went for them?" he asked.

"Ump," I replied; "he left us at the crossroads."

The man took his watch out of his pocket and studied for a moment. "Yes," he said, "you will get them."

It was put like some confident opinion based upon the arrival of an event.

"Mister Marsh," I said, "are you afraid of Ward? Isn't he good for the money?"

"Don't worry about that, my boy," he answered, taking up the candlestick, "I have said that you shall have the cattle, and you shall have them. Let me see about a bed for you."

Then he went out, closing the door after him.

I turned to Jud, and he pointed his finger to a letter lying on the mantelpiece. I arose and picked it up. It bore Cynthia's seal and was open.

Let us forgive little Miss Pandora. Old Jupiter ought to have known better. And the dimpled wife of Bluebeard! That forbidden door was so tremendously alluring!

I think I should have pulled the letter out of its envelope had I not feared that this man would return and find it in my fingers. I showed the seal to Jud and replaced it on the mantelpiece.

He slapped his leg. "Twiggs brought that," he said, "an' he's gone on to Westfall's. What does it say?"

"I didn't read it," I answered.

The man heaved his shoulders up almost to his ears. "Quiller," he said, "you can't root, if you have a silk nose."

I think I should have fallen, but at this moment Nicholas Marsh came back with his candle, and said we ought to sleep if we wished an early start in the morning. I followed him up the bare stairway to my room on the north side of the house. He placed the candlestick on the table, promised to call me early, then bade me good-night and went away.

I watched his broad back disappear in the shadow of the hall. Then I closed the door and latched it. Rigid honesty has its disadvantages. Here was a man almost persuaded to insist upon a right that was valid but unusual, and deeply worried because he had almost yielded to the urging. It takes good men to see the fine shades of such a thing.

There was a broad window in this room, with the bare limbs of the maples brushing against its casement. I looked out before I went to bed.

Beyond the Valley River, great smoky shadows cloaked the hills, gilded along their borders by the rising moon; hills that sat muffled in the foldings of their robes, waiting for the end,—waiting for man to play out the game and quit, and the Great Manager to pull down his scenery.

I blew out the candle, and presently slept as one sleeps when he is young. Sometime in the night I sat bolt upright in the good bed to listen. I had heard,—or was I dreaming,—floating up from some far distance, the last faint echo of that voice of Parson Peppers.

> "An' the ravens they did feed him, fare ye well,
> fare ye well."

I sprang out of bed and pressed my face against the window. There was no sound in the world. Below, the Valley River lay like a plate of burnished yellow metal. Under the enchanted moon it was the haunted water of the fairy. No mortal went singing down its flood, surely, unless he sailed in the ship that the tailors sewed together, or went a-dreaming in that mystic barge rowed by the fifty daughters of Danaus.

I crept back under the woven coverlid. This was haunted country, and Parson Peppers was doubtless snoring in a bed.

# CHAPTER XIII
# THE SIX HUNDRED

It is an unwritten law of the Hills that all cattle bought by the pound are to be weighed out of their beds, that is, in the early morning before they have begun to graze. This is the hour set by immemorial custom.

We were in the saddle while the sun was yet abed. The cattle were on two great boundaries of a thousand acres, sleeping in the deep blue grass on the flat hill-tops. Jud and two of Marsh's drivers took one line of the ridges, and Marsh and I took the other.

The night was lifting when we came out on the line of level hill-tops, and through the haze the sleeping cattle were a flock of squatting shadows. As we rode in among them the dozing bullocks arose awkwardly from their warm beds and stretched their great backs, not very well pleased to have their morning rest broken.

We rode about, bringing them into a bunch, arousing some morose old fellow who slept by himself in a corner of the hill, or a dozen aristocrats who held a bedchamber in some windless cove, or a straying Ishmaelite hidden in a broom-sedge hollow,—all displeased with the interruption of their forty winks before the sunrise. Was it not enough to begin one's day with the light and close it with the light? What did man mean by his everlasting inroads on the wholesome ways of nature? The Great Mother knew what she was about. All the people of the fields could get up in the morning without this cursed row. Whoever was one of them snoozing in his trundle-bed after the sun had flashed him a good morning?

The home-life of the steer would be healthy reading in any family. He never worries, and his temper has no shoal. Either he is contented and goes about his business, or he is angry and he fights. He is clean, and as regular in his habits as a lieutenant of infantry. To bed on the highlands when the dark comes, and out of it with the sun. A drink of water from the brook, and about to breakfast.

We gathered the cattle into a drove, and started them in a broken line across the hills toward the road, the huge black muleys strolling along, every fellow at his leisure. The sun peeping through his gateway in the east gilded the tops of the brown sedge and turned the grass into a sea of gold. Through this Eldorado the line of black cattle waded in deep grasses to the knee,—curly-coated beasts from some kingdom of the midnight in mighty contrast to this golden country. I might have been the Merchant's Son transported by some wicked fairy to a land of wonders, watching, with terror in his throat, the rebellious jins under some enchantment of King Solomon travelling eastward to the sun.

Now a hungry fellow paused to gather a bunch of the good-tasting grass and was butted out of the path, and now some curly-shouldered belligerent roared his defiant bellow and it went rumbling through the hills. We drove the cattle through the open gate of the pasture and down a long lane to the scales.

Nicholas Marsh seemed another man, and I felt the first touch of triumph come with the crisp morning. Woodford was losing. We had the cattle and there remained only to drive them in. It is a wonderful thing how the frost glistening on a rail, or a redbird chirping in a thicket of purple raspberry briers, can lift the heart into the sun. Marks and his crew were creatures of a nightmare, gone in the daylight, hung up in the dark hollow of some oak tree with the bat.

Marsh and the drivers went ahead of the cattle to the scales, and I followed the drove, stopping to close the gate and fasten it with its wooden pin to the old chestnut gate-post. High up on this gate-post was a worn hole about as big as a walnut, door to the mansion of some speckled woodpecker. As I whistled merrily under his sill, the master of this house stepped up to his threshold and leered down at me.

He looked old and immoral, with a mosaic past, the sort of woodpecker who, if born into a higher estate, would have guzzled rum and gambled with sailors. His head was bare in spots, his neck frowsy, and his eyelids scaly. "Young sir," this debauched old Worldly Wiseman seemed to say, "you think you're a devil of a fellow merely because it happens to be morning. Gad sooks! You must be very young. When you get a trifle further on with the mischief of living, you will realise that a bucketful of sunlight doesn't run the devil out of business. Damme, sirrah! Please to clear out with your accursed whistling."

I left him to cool his head in the morning breezes.

Nicholas Marsh was waiting for me at the scales when I arrived. He wished me to see that they were balanced properly. He adjusted the beam, adding a handful of shot or a nail or an iron washer to the weights. Then we put on the fifty-pound test, and then a horse. When we were satisfied that the scales were in working order, we weighed the cattle four at a time.

I took down the weights as Marsh called them, and when we had finished, the drove was turned into the road toward the river.

Marsh grasped my hand when I turned to leave him. "Quiller," he said, "it's hard to guard against a liar, but I do not believe there was ever a time when I would have refused you these cattle. Your brother has done me more than one conspicuous kindness. I would trust him for the cattle if he did not own an acre."

"Mr. Marsh," I said, "what lie did Woodford tell you?"

"I was told," he replied, "that Mr. Ward had transferred all of his land, and as these cattle would lose a great deal of money, he did not intend to pay this loss. I was shown a copy of the court record, or what purported to be one, to prove that statement. I do not think that I ever quite believed, but the proof seemed good, and I saw no reason for the lie."

He stopped a moment and swept the iron-grey locks back from his face. "Now," he continued, "I know the reason for that lie. And I know the paper shown me was spurious. It was high-handed rascality, but I cannot connect it with Woodford. It may have emanated from him, but I do not know that. The man who told me disclaimed any relation with him."

"Twiggs!" I said.

"No," he answered, "it was not Twiggs. The man was a heifer buyer from the north country. I would scarcely know him again."

"Not Twiggs!" I cried, "he was here last night."

"I know it," Marsh answered calmly. "He brought me this letter from Miss Cynthia. Will you carry it back to her, and say that your brother's word is good enough for Nicholas Marsh?"

He put his hand into his coat and handed me Cynthia's letter; and I stuffed it into my pockets without stopping to think. I tried to thank him for this splendid fidelity to Ward, but somehow I choked with the words pushing each other in my throat. He saw it, wished me a safe drive, and rode away to his house.

He was a type which the Hills will do ill to forget in the rearing of their sons, a man whose life was clean, and therefore a man difficult to wrong. I should have been sorry to stand before Nicholas Marsh with a lie in my mouth. He is gone now to the Country of the Silences. He was a just man, and to such, even the gods are accustomed to yield the wall.

I followed slowly after the drove, the broad dimensions of Woodford's plan at last clear in my youthful mind. He had put Ward in his bed, and out of the way. Then he had sent a stranger to these men with a dangerous lie corroborated by a bit of manufactured evidence,—a lie calculated to put any cattleman on his guard, and one that could not be tracked back to its sources.

Then, to make it sure, Twiggs had come riding like the devil's imps with some new warning from Cynthia. How could such planning fail? And failed it had not but for the honour of this gentleman, or perhaps some design of the Unknowable behind the machinery of the world.

Generation of intriguers! Here are the two factors that wreck you. The high captains of France overlooked the one in the prosecution of an obscure subordinate. And Absalom, the first great master of practical politics, somehow overlooked the other.

In my pocket was the evidence of Cynthia's perfidy, with the envelope opened, travelling home, as lies are said to. Ward might doubt the attitude of this woman when she smoothed matters with that dimpled mouth of hers, or crushed me out with her steel-grey eyes; but he would believe what she had written when he saw it. Then a doubt began to arise like the first vapour from the copper pot of the Arabian fisherman. Could I show it to Ward? Marsh had sent it to Cynthia. Could I even look at it? I postponed the contest with that genie.

Suicide is not a more deliberate business than cattle driving. A bullock must never be hurried, not even in the early morning. He must be kept strolling along no faster than he pleases. If he is hurried, one will presently have him panting with his tongue out, or down in a fence corner with the fat melted around his heart. Yet if he is allowed his natural gait, he will walk a horse to death.

Remember, he carries fifteen hundred pounds, and there are casks of tallow under his black hide. Besides that, he is an aristocrat accustomed to his ease. In large droves it is advisable to keep the herd in as long and narrow a line as possible, and to facilitate the driving, a few bullocks are usually separated from the others and kept moving in the van as a sort of pace-setter.

It is surprising how readily the drove falls into the spirit of this strolling march, some battle-scarred old bull leading, and the others following him in the dust.

It is said that neither fools, women, nor children can drive cattle. The explanation of this adage is not here assumed, nor its community of relation. I know the handling of these great droves is considered business for an expert. The cattle owner would no sooner trust a herd to men picked up by the roadway than the trainmaster would trust the limited express to a stranger in the railroad station.

If the cattle are hot they must be rested, in water if possible; if there is no water, then under some shade. Throw down the fence and turn them into the stranger's field. If the stranger is a person of good sense, he will be glad to assist your necessity. If not, he must yield to it.

These are laws of the Hills, always remembered as the lawyer remembers the "statute of frauds." It is impossible to go too slow. Watch the mouth of the bullock. He is in no danger until his tongue lolls out at the corner like a dog's. Then rest him. Let no man go through your drove. He must stop until it passes him. If he refuses, he must be persuaded. If one bullock runs back, let him alone; he will follow. But if two, turn them at once with a swift dash of the cattle-horse. Never run a steer. If the cattle are frightened, sing to them, and ride through the drove. Old-fashioned, swinging, Methodist hymns are best. Make it loud. The cattle are not particular about the tune.

I have heard the profane Ump singing Old Hundred and riding the Bay Eagle up and down in a bunch of frightened cattle, and it was a piece of comedy for the gods. I have heard Jud, with no more tune than a tom-tom, bellowing the doxology to a great audience of Polled-Angus muleys on the verge of a stampede. And I have sung myself, many a time, like a circuit rider with a crowded mourner's bench.

One thing more: know every bullock in your drove. Get his identity in your mind as you get the features of an acquaintance, so that you would recognise him instantly if you met him coming up at the end of the earth. A driver in the Hills would not be worth his salt who did not know every head of his cattle. Suppose his herd breaks into a field where there are others of the same breed, or he collides with another drove, or there is a tremendous mix at a tavern. The facility with which a cattle man learns to recognise every steer in a drove of hundreds is an eighth wonder of the world to a stranger. Anyone of us could ride through a drove of cattle, and when he reached the end know every steer that followed him in the road, and I have seen a line reaching for miles.

Easy with your eyebrows, my masters. When men are trained to a craft from the time they are able to cling to a saddle, they are very apt to exhibit a skill passing for witchcraft with the uninitiated. I have met many a grazier, and I have known but one who was unable to recognise the individual bullock in his drove, and his name was a byword in the Hills.

Jud and the Cardinal followed the drove, and I rode slowly through the cattle, partly to keep the long line thin, but chiefly to learn the identity of each steer. I looked for no mark, nor any especial feature of the bullock, but caught his identity in the total as the head waiter catches the identity of a hat. I looked down at each bullock for an instant, and then turned to the next one. In that instant I had the cast of his individuality forever. The magicians of Pharaoh could not afterwards mislead me about that bullock. This was not esoteric skill. Any man in the Hills could do it. Indeed it was a necessity. There was not a branded bullock in all this cattle land. What need for the barbaric custom when every man knew his cattle as he knew his children?

Later on, when little men came, at mid-life, to herding on the plains, they were compelled to burn a mark on their cattle. But we who had bred the beef steer for three-quarters of a century did no such child's play. How the crowd at Roy's tavern would have roared at such baby business. I have seen at this tavern a great mix of a dozen herds, that looked as like as a potful of peas, separated by an idle loafer sitting on a fence, calling out, "That one's Woodford's, an' that one's Alkire's an' that one's Maxwell's, an' the Polled-Angus muley belongs to Flave Davisson, an' the old-fashioned one is Westfield's. He must have got him in Roane or Nicholas. An' the Durham's Queen's, an' the big Holstein belongs to Mr. Ward, an' the red-faced Hereford is out of a Greenbrier cow an' goes with the Carper's."

By the time I had gotten through the drove we had reached the crossroads, and I found Ump waiting with the two hundred cattle of Westfall. The Bay Eagle was watching the steers, and Ump was sitting sidewise in his saddle with his hands around his knees.

I hailed him. "Did you have a hard job?"

"Easy as rollin' off a log," he answered. "I thought King David would throw his coat, but he was smooth-mouthed an' cross-legged as a peddler."

"Did Twiggs get in?" I asked.

"Beat me by a neck," answered the hunchback. "But I passed him comin' out an' I lit in to him."

"Fist and skull?" said I.

"Jaw," said he. "I damned every Carper into fiddlestrings from old Adam to old Columbus."

"What did he say?"

"He said we was the purtiest bunch of idiots in the kingdom of cowtails."

# CHAPTER XIV
# RELATING TO THE FIRST LIARS

The autumn in the Hills is but the afternoon of summer. The hour of the new guest is not yet. Still the heat lies on the earth and runs bubbling in the water. The little maid trots barefoot and the urchin goes a-swimming in the elm-hole by the corner of the meadow. Still the tender grass grows at the roots of the dead crop, and the little purple flowers dimple naked in the brown pasture. Still that Pied Piper of Hamelin, the everlasting Pan, flutes in the deep hollows, squatted down in the broom-sedge. And still the world is a land of unending summer, of unfading flowers, of undying youthfulness. Only for an hour or so, far in the deep night does the distant breath of the Frost King come to haunt the land, and then when the sun flings away his white samite coverlid it is summer again, with the earth shining and the water warm.

It was hot mid-morning when the long drove trailed down toward Horton's Ferry. The sweat was beginning to trickle in the hair of the fat cattle. Here and there through the herd a quarrelsome fellow was beginning to show the effect of his fighting and the heat. His eyes were a bit watery in his dusty face, and the tip of his tongue was slipping at his lips. The warm sun was getting into the backs of us all. I had stripped off my coat and carried it thrown across the horn of the saddle. Ump rode a mile away in the far front of the drove, keeping a few steers moving in the lead, while Jud shifted his horse up and down the long line. I followed on El Mahdi, lolling in the big saddle. Far away, I could hear Ump shout at some perverse steer climbing up against the high road bank, or the crack of Jud's driving whip drifted back to me. The lagging bullocks settled to the rear, and El Mahdi held them to the mark like a good sergeant of raw militiamen.

Ump and his leaders had reached the open common by the ferry when the long line stopped, and I saw Jud go to the front in a gallop. I waited for the column to go on, but it did not, and I began to drive the cattle in, bunching them up in the road.

Presently Jud came down into the turnpike and shouted to me. Then he dismounted, tied the reins around the horn of the saddle, and started the

Cardinal to the rear. The trained cattle-horse knew very well what he was to do, and picked his way through the steers until he reached me. Then he turned in the road, and I left him to watch the drove while I went to the front to see what the trouble was.

Both the Cardinal and the Bay Eagle were trained to this business and guarded the rear of the drove like dogs. The rider might lounge under a shade-tree, kicking up his heels to the sky. For this work El Mahdi was a trifle too eccentric, and we did not trust him.

Jud was gone when I reached the little bank where the road turned into the common of the ferry. I passed through the van of the cattle as they stood idly on the sodded open swinging their long tails with comfortable indifference. Then I came out where I could see the bank of the river and the blue smoke trailing up from the chimney of the ferrymen.

Facing the north at the front door of this house, Ump sat on the Bay Eagle, the reins down on the mare's neck and the hunchback's long hands crossed and resting on the horn of his saddle.

The attitude of the man struck me with a great fear. About him lurked the atmosphere of overwhelming defeat. The shadow of some mighty disaster loomed over against the almost tragic figure of the motionless hunchback sitting a horse of stone.

In such moments of strain the human mind has a mysterious capacity for trifles. I noticed a wisp of dry sedge bloom clinging to the man's shoulder,—a flimsy detail of the great picture.

The hunchback made no sign when I rode by him. What he had seen was still there beyond him in the sun. I had eyes; I could see.

On a stone by the landing sat one of the ferrymen, Danel, his hands in the pockets of his brown homespun coat. Neither Jud nor the other brother was anywhere in sight. I looked up at the steel cable above the man's head. It ended twenty feet away in the water.

I arose in the stirrups and searched the bank for the boat. It was gone. The Valley River ran full, a quarter of a mile of glistening yellow water, and no way across it but the way of the bass or the way of the heron.

The human mind has caves into which it can crawl, pits where it hides itself when it wishes to escape; dark holes leading back under the crags of the abyss. This explains the dazed appearance of one who is told suddenly of a disaster. The mind has crawled up into these fastnesses. For the time the distance is great between it and the body of the man through which it manifests itself. An enemy has threatened, and the master has gone to hide himself. The mind is a coward, afraid always of the not-mind. Like the frightened child, it must be given time to creep back to its abandoned plaything.

The full magnitude of this disaster to the ferry came slowly, as when one smooths out a crumpled map. In the great stillness I heard a wren twittering in the reeds along the bank, and I noted a green grasshopper, caught in the current, swimming for his life.

Then I saw it all to the very end, and I sickened. I felt as though some painless accident had removed all the portion of my body below the diaphragm. It was physical sickness. I doubled over and linked my fingers across my stomach, my head down almost to the saddle. Marks and his crew had done the work for us. The cable had been cut, and the boat had drifted away or been stolen. We were on the south side of the Valley River twirling our thumbs, while they rode back to their master with the answer, "It is done."

Then, suddenly, I recalled the singing which I had heard in the night. It was no dream, that singing. Peppers had stolen the boat and floated it away with the current. I could see Cynthia laughing with Hawk Rufe. Then I saw Ward, and the sickness left me, and the tears came streaming through my eyes. I put my arms down on the horn of the saddle and sobbed.

Remember, I was only a boy. Men old in the business of life become accustomed to loss; accustomed to fingers snatching away the gain which they have almost reached up to; accustomed to the staggering blow delivered by the Unforeseen. Like gamblers, they learn finally to look with indifference on the mask that may disguise the angel, or the death; on the curtain of to-morrow that may cover an Eldorado or a tomb. They come to see that the eternal forces are unknowable, following laws unknowable, from the seed sprouting in a handful of earth to the answer of a woman, "I do not love you."

But the child does not know the truth. He has been lied to from the cradle; taught a set of catchwords, a set of wise saws, a set of moral rules, logarithms by which the equation of life could be worked out, all arbitrary, and many grossly erroneous. He is led to believe that his father or the schoolmaster has grasped the scheme of human life and can explain it to him.

The nurse says it will come out all right, as though the Unforeseen could be determined by a secret in her possession. He is satisfied that these wise ones know. Then he meets the eternal forces, an event threatens, he marshals his catchwords, his wise saws, his moral rules, and they fail him. He retires, beaten, as the magicians of Egypt retired before God.

His father or the nurse or the schoolmaster explains with some outlandish fairy story, shifts the catchword or the saw or the rule, as a physician shifts the prescription of a consumptive, and returns him to the tremendous Reality. Again he spreads his hands and cries the sacred formula, the eternal forces advance, he stands fast and is flung bleeding to the wall, or he flees. Afraid, hidden in some cranny of the rocks, nursing his hurt, the child begins to see the truth. This passing from the world as it should be to the world as it is nearly kills him. It is like the riving of timber.

Presently I heard Jud speak to me from behind El Mahdi. The full strong voice of the man was like a dash of cold water in the face. I sat up; he bade me join Ump and himself to discuss what should be done, then turned around and went back to the house.

I slipped down from El Mahdi, washed my face in the river, and wiped it dry on my sleeve. Then I climbed into the saddle and rode back to where the little group stood before the door.

There were Ump and Jud, the two ferrymen, and their ancient mother. Danel was describing the catastrophe in a low voice, as one might describe the last illness of a man whose corpse was waiting in his house for burial.

"We set Twiggs over pretty late. Then there wasn't anybody else. So we tied up the boat an' went to bed. Mother sleeps by the fire. Mother has rheumatiz so she don't sleep very sound. About midnight she called me. She was sitting up in the bed with a shawl around her. 'Danel,' she said, 'there's something lumbering around the boat. Hadn't you better slip down an' see about it?' I told mother I reckoned it was a swimmin' tree. Sometimes they hit against the boat when they go down. Then I waked Mart up an' told him mother heard somethin' bumpin' against the boat, an' I reckoned it was a swimmin' tree. Mart was sleepy an' he said he reckoned it was. Then I turned over an' went to sleep again. When we got out this mornin', the cable was broke loose an' the boat swum off. We s'pose," here he paused and looked gravely at his brother, who as gravely nodded his head, "we s'pose the cable pulled loose somehow."

"It was cut in two," said I.

The ferryman screwed his head around on his neck as though he had not heard correctly. "Did you say 'cut in two'?" he repeated.

"Yes," said I, "cut in two. That cable was cut in two."

The man began to rub his chin with his hand. "I reckon not, Quiller," he said. "I reckon there ain't no person ornery enough to do that."

"It might be," piped the old woman, thrusting in. "There's been sich. Oncet, a long time ago, when your pap was a boy, goin' girlin' some, about when he begun a settin' up to me, a feller stole the ferryboat, but he was a terrible gallus feller."

"Granny," said Ump, "the devil ain't dead by a long shot. There is rapscallions lickin' plates over the Valley that's meaner than gar-broth. They could show the Old Scratch tricks that would make his eyes stick out so you could knock 'em off with a clapboard."

Danel protested. He pointed out that neither he nor his brother had ever done any man a wrong, and therefore no man would wrong them. It was one of those rules which children discover are strangely not true. He said the ferry was for the good of all, and therefore all would preserve rather than injure that good. Another wise saw, verbally sound, but going to pieces under the pitiless logic of fact.

This man, who had spent his life as one might spend it grinding at a mill, now, when he came to reckon with the natures of men, did it like a child. Ump cut him short. "Danel," he said, "you talk like a meetin'-house. Old Christian cut that cable with a cold chisel, an' Black Malan or Peppers stole your boat. They have nothing against you. They wanted to stop us from crossin' with these cattle, an' I guess they've done it."

Then he turned to me. The vapourings of the ferryman were of no importance. "Quiller," he said, "we're in the devil's own mess. What do you think about it?"

"I don't know," I answered; "what does Jud think?"

The face of the giant was covered with perspiration standing in beads. He clenched his hands and clamped his wet fists against the legs of his breeches. "God damn 'em!" he said. It was the most terrible oath that I have ever heard. Then he closed his mouth.

Ump looked at the man, then rode his horse over to me.

"Quiller," he said slowly, "we're gone up unless we can swim the drove across, an' it's a hell of a risky job. Do you see that big eddy?" and he pointed his finger to the middle of the Valley River where the yellow water swung around in a great circle. "If the steers bunched up in that hole, they'd drown like rats."

I looked at the wide water and it scared me. "Ump," I said, "how long could they stay in there without giving out?"

"They wouldn't give out," replied the hunchback, "if we could keep 'em above the eddy. A steer can swim as long as a horse if he ain't crowded. If we could keep 'em goin' in a long loop, we could cross 'em. If they bunched up, it would be good-bye, pap."

"Do you think they would grind in there if they happened to bunch?" said I.

"To kindlin'," responded Ump, "if they ever got at it good."

"Ump," I said, looking him squarely in the face, "I'm afraid of it."

The man chewed his thin upper lip. "So am I, Quiller," he answered. "But there ain't much choosin'; we either swim 'em or we go up the spout."

"Well," said I, "do we do it, or not do it?"

The hunchback studied the river. "Quiller," he said finally, "if we knowed about that current——"

I cut him short. "I'll find out about the current," I said. Then I threw away my hat, pitched my coat down on the sod and gathered up my bridle reins.

"Wait!" cried the hunchback. Then he turned to Jud. "Wash your face in the tub by the spout yonder, an' bring up your horse. Take Danel with you. Open Tolbert's fence an' put the cattle in the grove. Then come back here. Quiller's the lightest; he's goin' to try the current."

Then he swung around and clucked to the mare. I spoke to El Mahdi and we rode down toward the river. On the bank Ump stopped and looked out across the water, deep, wide, muddy. Then he turned to me.

"Hadn't you better ride the Bay Eagle?" he said. "She knows more in a minute than any horse that was ever born."

"What's wrong with El Mahdi?" I said, piqued a little.

"He ain't steady," responded the hunchback; "an' he knows more tricks than a meetin'-house rat. Sometimes he swims an' sometimes he don't swim, an' you can't tell till you git in."

"This," said I, "is a case of 'have to.' If he don't like the top, there's ground at the bottom." Then I kicked the false prophet in the flanks with my heels. The horse was standing on the edge of the sodded bank. When my heels struck him, he jumped as far as he could out into the river.

There was a great splash. The horse dropped like a stone, his legs stiff as ramrods, his neck doubled under and his back bowed. It was a bucking jump and meant going to the bottom. I felt the water rush up and close over my head.

I clamped my legs to the horse, held my breath, and went down in the saddle. I thought we should never reach the bottom of that river. The current tugged, trying to pull me loose and whirl me away. The horse under me felt like a millstone. The weight of water pressed like some tremendous thumb. Then we struck the rock bottom and began to come up. The sensation changed. I seemed now to be thrust violently from below against a weight pressing on my head, as though I were being used by some force under me to drive the containing cork out of the bottle in which we were enclosed. I began to be troubled for breath, my head rang. The distance seemed interminable. Then we popped up on the top of the river, and I filled with the blessed air to the very tips of my fingers.

The horse blew the water out of his nostrils and doubled his long legs. I thought he was going down again, and, seizing the top of the saddle horn, I loosed my feet in the stirrups. If El Mahdi returned to the deeps of that river, he would go by himself.

He stretched out his grey neck, sank until the water came running over the saddle, and then began to swim with long, graceful strokes of his iron legs as though it were the easiest thing in the world.

# CHAPTER XV
# WHEN PROVIDENCE IS PAGAN

The strength of the current did not seem to be so powerful as I had judged it. However, its determination was difficult. The horse swam with great ease, but he was an extraordinary horse, with a capacity for doing with this apparent ease everything which it pleased him to attempt. I do not know whether this arose from the stirring of larger powers ordinarily latent, or whether the horse's manner somehow concealed the amount of the effort. I think the former is more probable.

Half-way across the river, we were not more than twenty yards down-stream from the ferry landing. Ump shouted to turn down into the eddy, and I swung El Mahdi around. A dozen long strokes brought us into the almost quiet water of the great rim to this circle, a circle that was a hundred yards in diameter, in which the water moved from the circumference to the centre with a velocity increasing with the contracting of its orbit, from almost dead water in its rim to a whirling eddy in its centre.

I pulled El Mahdi up and let him drift with the motion of the water. We swung slowly around the circle, moving inward so gently that our progress was almost imperceptible.

The panic of men carried out in flood water can be easily understood. The activity of any power is very apt to alarm when that power is controlled by no intelligence. It is the unthinking nature of the force that strikes the terror. Death and the dark would lose much if they lost this attribute. The water bubbled over the saddle. The horse drifted like a chip. To my eyes, a few feet above this flood, the water seemed to lift on all sides, not unlike the sloping rim of some enormous yellow dish, in which I was moving gradually to the centre.

If I should strike out toward the shore, we should be swimming up-hill, while the current turning inward was apparently travelling down. This delusion of grade is well known to the swimmer. It is the chiefest terror of great water. Expert swimmers floating easily in flood water have been observed to turn over suddenly, throw up their arms, and go down. This is probably panic caused by believing themselves caught in the vortex of a cone, from which there seems no escape, except by the impossible one of swimming up to its rim, rising on all sides to the sky.

In a few minutes El Mahdi was in the centre of the eddy, carried by a current growing always stronger. In this centre the water boiled, but it was for the most part because of a lashing of surface currents. There seemed to be no heavy twist of the deep water into anything like a dangerous whirlpool. Still there was a pull, a tugging of the current to a centre. Again I was unable to estimate the power of this drag, as it was impossible to estimate how much resistance was being offered by the horse.

In the vortex of the eddy the delusion of the vast cone was more pronounced. It was one of the dangerous elements to be considered. I observed the horse closely to determine, if possible, whether he possessed this delusion. If he did, there was not the slightest evidence of it. He seemed to swim on the wide river with the indifference of floating timber, his head lying flat, and the yellow waves slipping over him to my waist. The sun beat into this mighty dish. Sometimes, when it caught the water at a proper angle, I was blinded and closed my eyes. Neither of these things seemed to give El Mahdi the slightest annoyance. I heard Ump shout and turned the horse toward the south shore. He swam straight out of the eddy with that same mysterious ease that characterised every effort of this eccentric animal, and headed for the bank of the river on the line of a bee. He struck the current beyond the dead water, turned a little up stream and came out on the sod not a hundred paces below the ferry. Both Ump and Jud rode down to meet me.

El Mahdi shook the clinging water from his hide and resumed his attitude of careless indifference.

"Great fathers!" exclaimed Jud, looking the horse over, "you ain't turned a hair on him. He ain't even blowed. It must be easy swimmin'."

"Don't fool yourself," said the hunchback. "You can't depend on that horse. He'd let on it was easy if it busted a girt."

"It was easy for him," I said, rising to the defence.

"Ho, ho," said Ump, "I wouldn't think you'd be throwin' bokays after that duckin'. I saw him. It wasn't so killin' easy."

"It couldn't be so bad," said Jud; "the horse ain't a bit winded."

"Laddiebuck," cried the hunchback, "you'll see before you get through. That current's bad."

I turned around in the saddle. "Then you're not going to put them in?" I said.

"Damn it!" said the hunchback, "we've got to put 'em in."

"Don't you think we'll get them over all right?" said I, bidding for the consolation of hope.

"God knows," answered the hunchback.

"It'll be the toughest sleddin' that we ever went up against." Then he turned his mare and rode back to the house of the ferrymen, and we followed him.

Ump stopped at the door and called to the old woman. "Granny," he said, "set us out a bite." Then he climbed down from the Bay Eagle, one leg at a time, as a spider might have done.

"Quiller," he called to me, "pull off your saddle, an' let Jud feed that long-legged son of a seacook. He'll float better with a full belly."

Jud dismounted from the Cardinal. "When does the dippin' begin?" he said. "Mornin' or afternoon service?"

The hunchback squinted at the sun. "It's eleven o'clock now," he answered. "In an hour we'll lock horns with Hawk Rufe an' hell an' high water, an' the devil keeps what he gits."

Jud took off the saddles and fed the horses shelled corn in the grass before the door, and after the frugal dinner we waited for an hour. The hunchback was a good general. When he went out to the desperate sally he would go with fresh men and fresh horses. I spent that hour on my back.

Across the road under the chestnut trees the black cattle rested in the shade, gathering strength for the long swim. On the sod before the door the horses rolled, turning entirely over with their feet in the air. Jud lay with his legs stretched out, his back to the earth, and his huge arms folded across his face.

Ump sat doubled up on the skirt of his saddle, his elbows in his lap, his long fingers linked together, and the shaggy hair straggling across his face. He was the king of the crooked men, planning his battle with the river while his lieutenants slept with their bellies to the sun.

I was moving in some swift dream when the stamping of the horses waked me and I jumped up. Jud was tightening the girth on El Mahdi. The Cardinal stood beside him bridled and saddled. Ump was sitting on the Bay Eagle, his coat and hat off, giving some order to the ferrymen who were starting to bring up the cattle. The hunchback was saving every breath of his horses. He looked like some dwarfish general of old times.

I climbed up on El Mahdi bareheaded, in my shirt sleeves, as I had ridden him before. Jud took off his coat and hat and threw them away. Then he pulled off his shirt, tied it in a knot to the saddle-ring, tightened the belt of his breeches, and got on his horse naked to the waist. It was the order of the hunchback.

"Throw 'em away," he said; "a breath in your horse will be worth all the duds you can git in a cart."

Danel and Mart laid down the fence and brought the cattle into the common by the ferry. Directed by the hunchback they moved the leaders of the drove around to the ferry landing. The great body of the cattle filled the open behind the house. The six hundred black muleys made the arc of a tremendous circle, swinging from the ferry landing around to the road. It was impossible to get farther up the river on this side because of a dense beech thicket running for a quarter of a mile above the open.

It was our plan to put the cattle in at the highest point, a few at a time, and thereby establish a continuous line across the river. If we could hold this line in a reasonable loop, we might hope to get over. If it broke and the cattle drifted down-stream we would probably never be able to get them out.

When the drove stood as the hunchback wished it, he rode down to the edge of the river, Jud and I following him. I felt the powerful influence exerted by the courage of this man. He leaned over and patted the silk shoulders of the Bay Eagle. "Good girl," he said, "good girl." It was like a last caress, a word spoken in the ear of the loved one on the verge of a struggle sure to be lost, the last whisper carrying all the devotion of a lifetime. Did the man at heart believe we could succeed? If the cattle were lost, did he expect to get out with his life? I think not.

Against this, the Cardinal and his huge naked rider contrasted strangely. They represented brute strength marching out with brute fearlessness into an unthinking struggle. Fellows and mates, these, the bronze giant and his horse. They might go under the yellow water of the Valley River, but it would be the last act of the last struggle.

As for me, I think I failed to realise the magnitude of this desperate move. I saw but hazily what the keen instinct of the hunchback saw so well,—all the possibilities of disaster. I went on that day as an aide goes with his general into a charge. I lacked the sense of understanding existing between the other men and their horses, but I had in its stead an all-powerful faith in the eccentric El Mahdi. No matter what happened, he would come out of it somehow.

Domestic cattle will usually follow a horse. It was the plan that I should go first, to lead fifty steers put in with me. Then Jud should follow to keep the bunch moving, while Ump and the two ferrymen fed the line, a few at a time, keeping it unbroken, and as thin as possible.

This was the only plan offering any shadow of hope. We could not swim the cattle in small bunches because each bunch would require one or two drivers, and the best horse would go down on his third trip. That course was out of the question, and this was the only other.

I think Ump had another object in putting me before the drove. If trouble came, I would not be caught in the tangle of cattle. I rode into the river, and they put the fifty leaders in behind me. This time El Mahdi lowered himself easily into the water and began to swim. I held him in as much as I could, and looked back over my shoulder.

The muleys dropped from the sod bank, went under to their black noses, came up, shook the water from their ears, and struck out, following the tail of the horse. They all swam deep, the water running across the middle of their backs, their long tails, the tips of their shoulders, and their quaint inky faces visible above the yellow water.

One after another they took the river until there were fifty behind me. Then Jud rode in, and the advance of the line was under way. Ump shouted to swing with the current as far as I could without getting into the eddy, and I forced El Mahdi gradually down-stream, holding his bit with both hands to make him swim as slow as he could.

We seemed to creep to the middle of the river. A Polled-Angus bullock with an irregular white streak running across his nose led the drove, following close at the horse's tail. That steer was Destiny. No criminal ever watched the face of his judge with more desperate interest than I watched the dish-face of that muley. I was now at the very middle of the river, and the turn must be made against the current. Would the steer follow me, or would he take the natural line of least resistance into the swinging water of the eddy? It was not a dozen yards below, whirling around to its boiling centre. The steer swam almost up to the horse's tail. I turned El Mahdi slowly against the current, and watched the black bullock over my shoulder. He turned after the horse. The current struck him in the deep forequarters; he swung out below the horse, threw his big chest to the current, and followed El Mahdi's tail like a fish following a bait. I arose in the stirrups and wiped the sweat off my face with my sleeve.

I could have shouted as I looked back. Jud and the fifty were turning the loop as though they were swinging at the end of a pendulum, every steer following his fellow like a sheep. Jud's red horse was the only bit of colour against that long line of black bobbing heads.

Behind him a string of swimming cattle reached in a long curve to the south bank of the Valley River. We moved slowly up the north curve of the long loop to the ferry landing. It was vastly harder swimming against the current, but the three-year-old steer is an animal of great strength. To know this, one has but to look at his deep shoulders and his massive brisket. The yellow water bubbled up over the backs of the cattle. The strong current swung their bodies around until their tails were down-stream, and the little waves danced in fantastic eddies around their puffing muzzles. But they clung to the crupper of El Mahdi with dogged tenacity, and when he climbed the north bank of the Valley River, the blazed face of the Polled-Angus leader came up out of the water at his heels.

I rode out on the good hard ground, and turned the horse's head toward the river. My heart sang and shouted under my shirt. The very joy of what I saw seemed to fill my throat choking full. The black heads dotted across the river might have been strung on a string. There were three hundred cattle in that water.

Jud and the first fifty were creeping up the last arm of the mighty curve, swimming together like brothers, the Cardinal sunk to his red head, and the naked body of his rider glistening in the sun.

When they reached the bank below me, I could restrain my joy no longer. I rose in the stirrups and whooped like the wildest savage that ever scalped a settler. I think the devil's imps sleeping somewhere must have heard that whooping.

# CHAPTER XVI
# THROUGH THE BIG WATER

Crowds of cattle, like mobs, are strangely subject to some sudden impulse. Any seamy-faced old drover will illustrate this fact with stories till midnight, telling how Alkire's cattle resting one morning on Bald Knob suddenly threw up their heads and went crashing for a mile through the underbrush; and how a line of Queen's steers charged on a summer evening and swept out every fence in the Tygart's valley, without a cause so far as the human eye could see and without a warning.

Three hundred cattle had crossed, swimming the track of the loop as though they were fenced into it, and I judge there were a hundred in the water, when the remainder of the drove on the south shore made a sudden bolt for the river. The move was so swift and uniform, and the distance to the water so short, that Ump and the ferrymen had barely time to escape being swept in with the steers. The whole drove piled up in the river and began to swim in a black mass toward the north shore. I saw the Bay Eagle sweep down the bank and plunge into the river below the cattle. I could hear Ump shouting, and could see the bay mare crowding the lower line of the swimming cattle.

The very light went out of the sky. We forced our horses into the river up to their shoulders, and waited. The cattle half-way across came out all right, but when the mass of more than two hundred reached the loop of the curve, they seemed to waver and crowd up in a bunch. I lost my head and plunged El Mahdi into the river. "Come on," I shouted, and Jud followed me.

If Satan had sent some guardian devil to choose for us an act of folly, he could not have chosen better than I. It is possible that the cattle would have taken the line of the leaders against the current if we had kept out of the river, but when they saw our horses they became bewildered, lost their sense of direction and drifted down into the eddy,—a great tangle of fighting cattle.

We swung down-stream, and taking a long circle came in below the drove as it drifted around in the outer orbit of the eddy. The crowd of cattle swam past, butting each other, and churning the water under their bellies, led by a half-blood Aberdeen-Angus steer with a ring in his nose. Half-way around we met Ump. He was a terrible creature. His shirt was in ribbons, and his hair was matted to his head. He was trying to force the Bay Eagle into the mass of cattle, and he was cursing like a fiend.

I have already said that his mare knew more than any other animal in the Hills. She dodged here and there like a water rat, slipped in among the cattle and shot out when they swung together. On any other horse the hunchback would have been crushed to pulp.

We joined him and tried to drive a wedge through the great tangle to split it in half, Jud and the huge Cardinal for a centre. We got half-way in and were flung off like a plank.

We floated down into the rim of the eddy below the cattle, spread out, and endeavoured to force the drove up stream. We might as well have ridden against a floating log-jam. The mad, bellowing steers swam after their leader, moving in toward the vortex of the eddy. The half-blood Aberdeen-Angus, whom the cattle seemed to follow, was now on the inner border of the drove, the tangle of steers stretched in a circle around him. It was clear that in a very few minutes he would reach the centre, the mass of cattle would crowd down on him, and the whole bunch would go to the bottom. We determined to make another effort to break through this circle, and if possible capture the half-blood and force him out toward the shore. A more dangerous undertaking could not be easily imagined.

The chances of driving this steer out were slight if we should ever reach him. The possibility of forcing a way in was remote, and if we succeeded in penetrating to the centre of the jam and failed to break it, we should certainly be wedged in and crushed. If Ump's head had been cool, I do not think he would ever have permitted me to join in such madness. We were to select a loose place in the circle, the Cardinal and El Mahdi to force an opening, and the Bay Eagle to go through if she could.

We waited while the cattle passed, bellowing and thrashing the water,—an awful mob of steers in panic. Presently in this circle there was a rift where a bull, infuriated by the crowding, swam by, fighting to clear a place around him. He was a tremendous creature, glistening black, active and dangerous as a wild beast. He charged the cattle around him, driving them back like a battering ram. He dived and butted and roared like some sea monster gone mad. Ump shouted, and we swam into the open rift against this bull, Jud leading, and El Mahdi at his shoulder.

The bull fighting the cattle behind him did not see us until the big sorrel was against him. Then he swung half around and tried to butt. This was the danger which we feared most. The ram of a muley steer is one of the most powerful blows delivered by any animal. For this reason, no bull with horns is a match for a muley. The driving power of sixteen hundred pounds of bone and muscle is like the ram of a ship. Striking a horse fair, it would stave him in as one breaks an egg shell. Jud leaned down from his horse and struck the bull on the nose with his fist, beating him in the nostrils. The bull turned and charged the cattle behind him. We crowded against him, using the mad bull for a great driving wedge.

I have never seen anything in the world to approach the strength or the fury of this muley. With him we broke through the circle of steers forcing into the centre of the eddy. We had barely room for the horses by crowding shoulder to shoulder to the bull. The cattle closed in behind us like bees swarming in a hive.

I was accustomed to cattle all my life. I had been among them when they fought each other, bellowing and tearing up the sod; among them when they charged; among them when they stampeded; and I was not afraid. But this caldron of boiling yellow water filled with cattle was a hell-pot. In it every steer, gone mad, seemed to be fighting for dear life.

I caught something of the terror of the cattle, and on the instant the delusion of the cone rising on all sides returned. The cattle seemed to be swarming down upon us from the sides of this yellow pit. I looked around. The Bay Eagle was squeezing against El Mahdi. Jud was pressing close to the nose of the bull, keeping him turned against the cattle by great blows rained on his muzzle, and we were driving slowly in like a glut.

My mouth became suddenly dry to the root of my tongue. I dropped the reins and whirled around in the saddle. Ump, whose knee was against El Mahdi's flank, reached over and caught me by the shoulder. The grip of his hand was firm and steady, and it brought me back to my senses, but his face will not be whiter when they lay him finally in the little chapel at Mount Horeb.

As I turned and gathered up the reins, the water was boiling over the horses. Sometimes we went down to the chin, the horses entirely under; at other times we were flung up almost out of the water by the surging of the cattle. The Cardinal was beginning to grow tired. He had just swam across the river and half-way back, and been then forced into this tremendous struggle without time to gather his breath. He was a horse of gigantic stature and great endurance, but his rider was heavy. He had been long in the water, and the jamming of the cattle was enough to wear out a horse built of ship timber.

His whole body was sunk to the nose and he went entirely under with every surge of the bull. The naked back of Jud reeked with sweat, washed off every minute with a flood of muddy water, and the muscles on his huge shoulders looked like folds of brass.

He held the bridle-rein in his teeth and bent down over the saddle so as to strike the bull when it tried to turn back. At times the man, horse, and bull were carried down out of sight.

Suddenly I realised that we were on the inside. The river was a bedlam of roars and bellows. We had broken through the circle of cattle, and it drifted now in two segments, crowding in to follow the half-blood Aberdeen-Angus. This steer passed a few yards below us, making for the centre of the eddy. As he went by, Ump shot out on the Bay Eagle, dodged through the cattle, and, coming up with the steer, reached down and hooked his finger in the ring which the half-blood wore in his nose. Then, holding the steer's muzzle against the shoulder of the mare, he struck out straight through the vortex of the eddy, making for the widest opening in the broken circle.

I watched the hunchback breathless. It was not difficult to lead the steer. An urchin could have done it with a rope in the nosering, but the two segments of the circle might swing together at any moment, and if they did Ump would be penned in and lost and we would be lost also, locked up in this jam of steers.

For a moment the hunchback and the steer passed out of sight in the boiling eddy, then they reached the open, went through it, and struck up-stream for the ferry landing.

The cattle on the inner side of the circle followed the Aberdeen-Angus, streaming through the opening in a great wedge that split the jam into the two wings of an enormous V. The whole drove swung out and followed in two lines, as one has seen the wild geese following their pilot to the south.

Jud and I, wedged in, were tossed about by the surging of the cattle, as the jam broke. We were protected a little by the bull, whose strength seemed inexhaustible. Every moment I looked to see some black head rise under the fore quarters of El Mahdi, throw him over, and force him down beneath the bellies of the cattle, or some muley charge the fighting bull and crush Jud and his horse. But the very closeness of the jamming saved us from these dangers.

It was almost impossible for a bullock to turn. We were carried forward by the press as a child is carried with a crowd. When the cattle split into the wings of the V, we were flung off and found ourselves swimming in open water between the two great lines.

I felt like a man lifted suddenly from a dungeon into the sunlit world. I was weak. I caught hold of the horn, settled down nerveless in the saddle, and looked around me. The cattle were streaming past in two long lines for the shore, led by Ump and the Aberdeen-Angus, now half-way up the north arm of the loop.

The river was still roaring with the bellowings of the cattle, as though all the devils of the water howled with fury at this losing of their prey.

The steers had now room to swim in, and they would reach the shore. I looked down at El Mahdi. He floated easily, pumping the air far back into his big lungs. He had been roundly jammed, but he was not exhausted, and I knew he would be all right when he got his breath.

Then I looked for Jud. He was a few yards below me, staring at the swimming cattle. The water was rising to his armpits. It poured over the Cardinal, and over the saddle horn. It was plain that the horse was going down. Only his muzzle hung above the water, with the nostrils distended.

I shouted to Jud. He kicked his feet out of the stirrups, dropped into the water and caught his horse by the shank of the bit. He went down until the water bubbled against his chin. But he held the horse's head above the river, treading water and striking out with his free arm.

I turned El Mahdi and swam to the Cardinal. When I reached him I caught the bit on my side, and together Jud and El Mahdi held the exhausted horse until he gathered his breath and began to swim. Presently, when he had gotten the air back in his chest, I took the bridle-rein, and Jud, loosing his hold on the bit, floated down behind the cattle, and struck out for the shore. I saw him climb the bank among the water beeches when El Mahdi and the Cardinal came up out of the river at the ferry landing behind the last bullock.

# CHAPTER XVII
# ALONG THE HICKORY RIDGES

The human analyst, jotting down in his note-book the motives of men, is often strangely misled. The master of a great financial house, working day and night in an office, is not trading away his life for a system of railroads. Bless you! sir, he would not give a day of those precious hours for all the steel rails in the world. Nor is my lady spending her life like water to reach the vantage-point where she may entertain Sir Henry. That tall, keen-eyed woman with the brains crowded in her head does not care a snap of her finger if the thing called Sir Henry be flying to the devil.

Look you a little further in, good analyst. It is the passion of the chess-player. Each of these is up to the shoulders in the grandest game you ever dreamed of. Other skilful men and other quick-witted women are there across the table with Chance a-meddling. The big plan must be carried out. The iron trumpery and the social folderol are bits of stuff that have to be juggled about in this business. They have no more intrinsic value than a bank of fog. Providence made a trifling miscalculation when it put together the human mind. As the thing works, there is nothing worth while but the thrills of the game. And these thrills! How they do play the devil with the candle! Thus it comes about that when one pulls his life or his string of playthings out of a hole he does not seem to have made a gain by it. I learned this on the north bank of the Valley River, listening to Ump's growls as he ran his hands over the Bay Eagle, and the replies of Jud lying by the Cardinal in the sun.

Gratitude toward the man helper is about as rare as the splinters of the true cross. When one owes the debt to Providence, one depends always upon the statute of limitations to bar it. Here sat these grateful gentlemen, lately returned by a sort of miracle to the carpet of the green sod, swapping gibes like a couple of pirates.

"Old Nick was grabbin' for us this time," said Jud, "an' he mighty nigh got us."

"I reckon," answered Ump, "a feller ought to git down on his marrow-bones."

"I wouldn't try it," said Jud. "You might cork yourself."

"It was like the Red Sea," said I; "all the cattle piled up in there, and going round and round."

"Just like the good book tells about it," added Ump; "only we was them Egyptians, a-flounderin' an' a-spittin' water."

"Boys," said Jud, "that Pharaoh-king ought to a been bored for the holler horn. I've thought of it often."

"Why?" I asked.

"You see," he answered, "after all them miracles, locusts, an' frogs an' sich, he might a knowed the Lord was a-layin' for him. An' when he saw that water piled up, he ought a lit out for home. 'Stead of that, he went asailin' in like the unthinkin' horse."

The hunchback cocked his eye and began to whistle. Then he broke into a ditty:

"When Pharaoh rode down to the ragin' Red Sea,
Rode down to the ragin' Red Sea,
He hollered to Moses, 'Just git on to me,
A-ridin' along through the sea.'

"An' Moses he answered to hollerin' Pharaoh,
The same as you'd answer to me,
'You'll have to have bladders tied on to your back,
If you ever git out of the sea.'"

Thus I learned that the man animal long ago knocked Young Gratitude on the head, heaved him overboard into a leaky gig, and left him behind to ogle the seagulls. He is a healthy pirate, this man animal, accustomed with great complacency to maroon the trustful stowaway when he comes to nose about the cargo of his brig, or thrusts his pleading in between the cutthroat and his pleasant sins.

As for me, I was desperately glad to be safe out of that pot of muddy water. I was ready like the apostle of old time to build here a tabernacle, or to go down on what Ump called my "marrow-bones." As it was, I dismounted and hugged El Mahdi, covering up in his wet mane a bit of trickling moisture strangely like those tears that kept getting in the way of my being a man.

I had tried to laugh, and it went string-halt. I had tried to take a hand in the passing gibes, and the part limped. I had to do something, and this was my most dignified emotional play. The blue laws of the Hills gave this licence. A fellow might palaver over his horse when he took a jolt in the bulwarks of his emotion. You, my younger brethren of the great towns, when you knock your heads against some corner of the world and go a-bawling to your mother's petticoat, will never know what deeps of consolation are to be gotten out of hugging a horse when one's heart is aching.

I wondered if it were all entirely true, or whether I should knock my elbow against something and wake up. We were on the north bank of the Valley River, with every head of those six hundred steers. Out there they were, strung along the road, shaking their wet coats like a lot of woolly dogs, and the afternoon sun wavering about on their shiny backs. And there was Ump with his thumbs against the fetlocks of the Bay Eagle, and Jud trying to get his copper skin into the half-dried shirt, and the hugged El Mahdi staring away at the brown hills as though he were everlastingly bored.

I climbed up into the saddle to keep from executing a fiddler's jig, and thereby proving that I suffered deeply from the curable disease of youth.

We started the drove across the hills toward Roy's tavern, Jud at his place in front of the steers, walking in the road with the Cardinal's bridle under his arm, and Ump behind, while El Mahdi strayed through the line of cattle to keep them moving. The steers trailed along the road between the rows of rail fence running in zigzag over the country to the north. I sat sidewise in my big saddle dangling my heels.

There were long shadows creeping eastward in the cool hollows when we came to the shop of old Christian the blacksmith. I was moving along in front of the drove, fingering El Mahdi's mane and whistling lustily, and I squared him in the crossroads to turn the plodding cattle down toward Roy's tavern. I noticed that the door of the smith's shop was closed and the smoke creeping in a thin line out of the mud top of the chimney, but I did not stop to inquire if the smith were about his work. I held no resentment against the man. He had doubtless cut the cable, as Ump had said, but his provocation had been great.

The settlement was now made fair, skin for skin, as the devil put it once upon a time. I whistled away and counted the bullocks as they went strolling by me, indicating each fellow with my finger. Presently Ump came at the tail of the drove and pulled up the Bay Eagle under the tall hickories.

"Well," he said, "the old shikepoke must be snoozin'."

"It's pretty late in the day," said I.

"He lost a lot of sleep last night," responded Ump. "When a feller travels with the devil in the night, he can't work with the Lord in the day."

"He hasn't been at it long," said I, pointing to the faint smoke hovering above the chimney; "or the fire would be out."

"Right," said Ump. "An, that's a horse of another colour. I think I shall take a look."

With that he swung down from his saddle, crossed to the shop, and flung open the door. Then he began to whistle softly.

"Hot nest," he said, "but no sign of the shikepoke."

"He may be hiding out until we pass," said I.

"Not he," responded the hunchback.

Then I took an inspiration. "Ump," I cried, "I'll bet the bit out of the bridle that he saw us coming and lit out to carry the word!"

The hunchback struck his fist against the door of the shop. "Quiller," he said, "you ought to have sideboards on your noggin. That's what he's done, sure as the Lord made little apples!"

Then he got on his horse and rode her through the hickories out to the brow of the hill. Presently I heard him call, and went to him with El Mahdi on a trot. He pointed his finger north across the country and, following the pointed finger, I saw the brown coat of a man disappearing behind a distant ridge. It was too far away to see who it was that travelled in that coat, but we knew as well as though the man's face had passed by our stirrups.

"Hoity-toity!" said Ump, "what doin's there'll be when he gits in with the news!"

"The air will be blue," said I.

"Streaked and striped," said he.

"I should like to see Woodford champing the bit," said I.

"I'd give a leg for the sight of it," replied the hunchback, "an' they could pick the leg."

I laughed at the hunchback's offer to the Eternal Powers. Of all the generation of rogues, he was least fitted to barter away his underpinning.

We rode back to the shop and down the hill after the cattle, Ump drumming on the pommel with his fingers and firing a cackle of fantastic monologue. "Quiller," he said, "do you think Miss Cynthia will be glad to see the drove comin' down the road?"

"Happy as a June bug," said I.

"Old Granny Lanham," continued the hunchback, "used to have a song that went like this:

"'God made man, an' man made money;
God made bees, an' bees made honey;
God made woman, an' went away to rest Him,
An' along come the devil, an' showed her how to best
Him.'"

"Meaning what?" said I.

"Meanin'," responded Ump, "that if you think you know what a woman's goin' to do, you're as badly fooled as if you burned your shirt."

"Ump," I said sharply, "what do you know about women?"

"Nothin' at all," said he, "nothin' at all. But I know about mares. An' when they lay back their ears, it don't always mean that they're goin' to kick you."

# CHAPTER XVIII
# BY THE LIGHT OF A LANTERN

It was a hungry, bareheaded youngster that rode up at sundown to Roy's tavern. The yellow mud clinging to my clothes had dried in cakes, and as my hat was on the other side of the Valley River, my head, as described by Ump, was a "middlin' fair brush heap."

Adam Roy gaped in astonishment when I called him to the door to ask about a field for the cattle.

"Law! Quiller," he cried, "where in the name o' fathers have you been a-wallerin'?"

"We went swimming in the Valley," I answered.

"Mercy sakes!" said the tavern-keeper, "you must a mired down. You've got mud enough on you to daub a chimney, an' your head looks like a chaff-pen on a windy mornin'. What did you go swimmin' for?"

"Hobson's choice," said I.

"Was the ferry washed out?" he asked.

"It was out," I said. "How it got out is a heifer of another drove."

"An' did you swim the cattle?" The man leaned out of the door.

I pointed my finger to the drove coming down the road. "There they are," said I. "Do you see any wings on them?"

"Lord love me!" cried the tavern-keeper, "I'd never put cattle in the Valley when it was up, unless I wanted to see their tails a stickin' out o' the drift-wood. Why didn't you wait until they fixed the ferry? What was your hurry?"

"No matter about that hurry," said I. "Just now we have another hurry that is a trifle more urgent. We want a field for the cattle, and corn and clover hay and plenty of bedding for the horses, and something hot for supper. We are all as hungry as Job's turkey."

"One thing at a time, Quiller," said the man, spreading his hands. "Turn the cattle into the north boundary an' come along to the house."

I went back up the road, threw down the bars to the pasture, and counted the cattle as they went strolling in. The Polled-Angus muleys seemed none the worse for their long swim, and they began to crop the brown grass the moment they were out in the field.

Jud and the Cardinal came up after the first hundred, and took a place by El Mahdi.

I think I know now the joy of the miser counting his gold pieces at midnight in his cellar, looking at each yellow eagle lovingly, and passing his finger over the milled rim of each new-minted coin, while the tallow candle melts down on the bench beside him.

I could close my eyes and see a black mass going down in the yellow water, with here and there a bullock drifting exhausted in the eddy, or heaps of bloated bodies piled up on a sandbar of the Valley River. And there, with my eyes wide open, was the drove spreading out along the hillside as it passed in between the two chestnut bar-posts.

I was as happy as a man can be when his Armada sails in with its sunlit canvas; and yet, had that Armada gone to pieces on a coast, I think my tears over its wreckage had been the deeper emotion. Our conception of disaster outrides by far our conception of felicity.

It is a thing of striking significance that old, wise poets have on occasion written of hell so vividly that we hear the fire crackle and see the bodies of the lost sizzling; but not one of them, burning the candle of genius at both ends, has ever been able to line out a heaven that a man would live in if he were given the key to it.

Ump came along after the last of the cattle and burst into a great laugh. "Damme," he said, "you're as purty a pair of muskrats as ever chawed a root. Why don't you put up the bars instead of settin' gawkin' at the cattle! They're all there."

"Suppose they were not all there?" said I.

"Quiller," said he, "I'm not goin' back over any burnt bridges. When the devil throws a man in a sink hole an' the Lord comes along an' pulls him out, that man ought to go on about his business an' not hang around the place until the devil gits back."

Jud got down from his horse and began to lay up the bars. "But," said he, "suppose we hadn't split the bunch?"

"Jud," answered the hunchback, "hell's full of people who spent their lives a-'sposin'."

Jud jammed the top bar into the chestnut post. "Still," he persisted, "where would we a been now?"

"If you must know," said Ump, "we'd a been heels up in the slime of the Valley with the catfish playin' pussy-in-the-corner around the butt of our ears."

We trotted over to the tavern, flung the bridle-reins across the hitching post, and went bursting into the house. Roy was wiping his oak table. "Mother Hubbard," cried the hunchback, "set out your bones. We're as empty as bee gums."

The man stopped with his hands resting on the cloth. "God save us!" he said, "if you eat like you look, it'll take a barbecue bull to fill you. Draw up a chair an' we'll give you what we've got."

"Horses first," said Ump, taking up a split basket.

"Suit yourself," said Roy; "there's nobody holdin' you, an' there's corn in the crib, hay in the mow, an' oats in the entry."

Jud and I followed Ump out of the house, put the horses in the log stable, pulled off the bridles and saddles, and crammed the racks with the sweet-smelling clover hay. Then we brushed out the mangers and threw in the white corn. When we were done we went swaggering back to the house.

From threatened disaster we had come desperately ashore. Whence arises the strange pride of him who by sheer accident slips through the fingers of Destiny?

We ate our supper under the onslaughts of the tavern-keeper. Roy had a mind to know why we hurried. He scented some reason skulking in the background, and he beat across the field like a setter.

"You'll want to get out early," he said. "Men who swim cattle won't be lettin' grass grow under their feet."

"Bright an' early," replied Ump.

"It appears like," continued Roy, "you mightn't have time enough to get where you're goin'."

"Few of us have," replied Ump. "About the time a feller gits a good start, somethin' breaks in him an' they nail him up in quarter oak."

"Life is short," murmured the tavern-keeper, retiring behind a platitude as a skirmisher retires behind a stone.

Ump bent the prongs of the fork against his plate. "An' yit," he soliloquised, "there is time enough for most of us to do things that we ought to be hung for."

Roy withdrew to the fastnesses of the kitchen, re-formed his lines and approached from another quarter. "If I was Mr. Ward," he opened, jerking his thumb toward Ump, "I'd give it to you when you got in."

The hunchback poured out his coffee, held up the saucer with both hands and blew away the heat. "What for?" he grunted, between the puffings.

"What for?" said Roy. "Lordy! man, you're about the most reckless creature that ever set on hog leather."

"The devil you say!" said Ump.

"That's what I say," continued the tavern-keeper, waving his arm to add fury to his bad declamation. "That's what I say. Suppose you'd got little Quiller drownded?"

The hunchback seemed to consider this possibility with the gravity of one pointed suddenly to some defect in his life. He replaced the saucer on the table, locked his fingers and thrust his thumbs together.

"If had got little Quiller drownded," he began, "then the old women couldn't a said when he growed up, 'Eh, little Quiller didn't amount to much after all. I said he wouldn't come to no good when I used to see him goin' by runnin' his horse.' An' when he got whiskers to growin' on his jaw, flat-nose niggers fishin' along the creek couldn't a' cussed an' said, 'There goes old skinflint Quiller. I wish he couldn't swallow till he give me half his land.' An' when he got old an' wobbly on his legs, tow-headed brats a-waitin' for his money couldn't a-p'inted their fingers at him an' said, 'Ma, how old's grandpap?' An' when he died, nobody could a wrote on his tombstone, 'He robbed the poor an' he cheated the rich, an' he's gone to hell with the balance a' sich.'"

Routed in his second man[oe]uvre, Roy flung a final sally with a sort of servile abandon. "You're a queer lot," he said. "Marks an' that club-footed Malan comes along away before day an' wants their breakfast, an' gits it, an' lights out like the devil was a-follerin' 'em. An' when I asked 'em what they'd been doin', they up an' says they'd been fixin' lay-overs to ketch meddlers an' make fiddlers' wives ask questions. An' then along come you all a-lookin' like hell an' shyin' at questions."

We took the information with no sign, although it confirmed our theory about the ferry. Ump turned gravely to the tavern-keeper.

"I'll clear it all up for you slick as a whistle." Then he arose and pressed his fingers against the tavern-keeper's chest. "Roy," he said, "this is the marrow out of that bone. We're the meddlers that they didn't ketch, an' you're the fiddler's wife."

The laughter sent the tavern-keeper flying from the field. We borrowed some odd pieces of clothing, got the lantern, and went down to the stable to groom our horses.

A man might travel about quite as untidy as Nebuchadnezzar when events were jamming him, but his horse was rubbed and cleaned if the heavens tumbled. I held the lantern, an old iron frame with glass sides, while Jud and Ump curried the horses, rubbing the dust out of their hair, and washing their eyes and nostrils.

We were speculating on the mission of the blacksmith, and the destination of Parson Peppers, of whose singing I had told, when the talk came finally to Twiggs.

"I'd give a purty," said Ump, "to know what word that devil was carryin'."

"Quiller had a chance to find out," answered Jud, "an' he shied away from it."

"What's that?" cried the hunchback, coming out from under the Bay Eagle. He wore a long blue coat that dragged the ground, the sleeves rolled up above his wrists, a coat that Roy had fished out of a box in the loft of his tavern and hesitated over, because on an evening in his youthful heyday, he had gone in that coat to make a bride of a certain Mathilda, and the said Mathilda at the final moment did most stubbornly refuse. The coat had brass buttons, a plenteous pitting of moth-holes, and a braided collar.

Jud went on without noticing the interruption. "The letter that Twiggs brought was a-layin' on the mantelpiece, tore open. Quiller could a looked just as easy as not, an' a found out just what it said, but he edged off."

The hunchback turned around in his blue coat without disturbing the swallowtails lying against his legs. "Is Jud right?" he said.

I nodded my head.

"An' you didn't look?"

Again I nodded.

"Quiller," cried Ump, "do you know how that way of talkin' started? The devil was the daddy of it. He had his mouth crammed full of souls, an' when they asked him if he wanted any more, he begun a-bobbin' his head like that."

"It's every word the truth," said I. "There was the letter lying open, with Cynthia's monogram on the envelope, and I could have looked."

"Why didn't you?" said Ump.

"High frollickin' notions," responded Jud. "I told him a hog couldn't root with a silk nose."

The hunchback closed his hand and pressed his thumb up under his chin. "High frollickin' notions," he said, "are all mighty purty to make meetin'-house talk, but they're short horses when you try to ride 'em. It all depends on where you're at. If you're settin' up to the Lord's table, you must dip with your spoon, but if you're suppin' with the devil, you can eat with your fingers."

I cast about for an excuse, like a lad under the smarting charge of having said his prayers. "It wasn't any notion," said I; "Mr. Marsh came back too quick."

"Why didn't you yank the paper, an' we'd a had it," said he.

"We have got it," said I, putting my hand in my breeches pocket and drawing forth the letter. I stood deep in the oak leaves of the horses' bedding. The light of the candle squeezing through the dirty glass sides brought every log of the old stable into shadow.

Jud came out of El Mahdi's stall like something out of a hole. He wore a rubber coat that had gone many years about the world, up and down, and finally passed in its decay to Roy.

"You've got that letter?" he said.

I told him that I had the very letter, that it had got wet in the river; I had dried it in the sun, and here it was.

"How did you get it?" he asked.

I told him all the conversation with Marsh, and how I was to give it to Cynthia and the message that went along with it.

The two men came over to me and took the lantern and the letter from my hands, Jud holding the light and Ump turning the envelope around in his fingers, peering curiously. They might have been some guardians of a twilight country examining a mysterious passport signed right but writ in cipher, and one that from some hidden angle might be clear enough.

Presently they handed the letter gravely back to me and set the lantern down in the leaves. Jud was silent, like a man embarrassed, and Ump stood for a moment fingering the buttons on his blue coat.

Finally he spoke. "What's in it?" he said.

"I don't know," I answered. I was sure that the man's face brightened, but it might have been a fancy. Loud in the hooting of a principle, we sometimes change mightily when it comes to breaking that principle bare-handed.

"Are you goin' to look?" he said.

The letter was lying in my hand. I had but to plunge my fingers into the open envelope, but something took me by the shoulder. "No," I answered, and thrust the envelope in my pocket.

I take no airs for that decision. There was something here that these men did not like to handle, and, in plain terms, I was afraid.

# CHAPTER XIX
# THE ORBIT OF THE DWARFS

We slept that night in the front room of Roy's tavern, and it seemed to me that I had just closed my eyes when I opened them again. Ump was standing by the side of the bed with a candle. The door was ajar and the night air blowing the flame, which he was screening with his hand. For a moment, with sleep thick in my eyes, I did not know who it was in the blue coat. "Wake up, Quiller," he said, "an' git into your duds."

"What's the matter?" I asked.

"There's devilment hatchin', I'm afraid," he answered. "Wait till I wake Jud."

He aroused the man from his snoring in the chimney corner, and I got into my clothes. It was about three o'clock and grey dark. I looked over the room as I pulled on the roundabout borrowed of Roy. Ump's bed had not been slept in, and there was about him the warm smell of a horse.

Jud noticed the empty bed. "Ump," he said, "you ain't been asleep at all."

"I got uneasy about the cattle," answered the hunchback, "an I've been up there with 'em, an' it was dam' lucky. I was settin' on the Bay Eagle in a little holler, when somebody come along an' begun to take down the bars. I lit out for him, an' he run like a whitehead, jumped the fence on the lower side of the road an' went splashin' through the creek, but he left some feathers in the bushes when he jumped, an' I got 'em."

He put his hand into the bosom of his coat and drew out a leather cap. "Christian," I cried, pointing to the seared spots on the leather.

Jud crushed the cap in his fingers. "He's got back," he said. "Was he ridin' a horse?"

"Footin' it," answered Ump, "an' by himself. That's what makes me leary. Them others are up to somethin' or they'd a come with him. He's had just about time to make the trip on Shank's mare by takin' short cuts. They've put him up to turn out the cattle an' drive 'em back while we snoozed."

"Maybe they did come with him," said Jud, "an' they're waitin' somewhere. It would be like 'em to come sneakin' back an' try to drive the cattle over, an' put 'em in the river in the night, so it would look like they had got out an' gone away themselves."

Ump's forehead wrinkled like an accordion. "That's fittin' to the size of 'em," he said, "an' about what they're up to. But old Christian was surely by himself, an' I don't understand that. If they'd a come with him, I'd a seen 'em, or a heard the horses."

"I don't believe they came with him," said I.

"Why not?" said Jud.

"Because," I answered, "if they came with him they would have put Christian on a horse, and they would have stopped here to locate us. They could tell by looking in the stable. They'd never wait until they got to the field. They're a foxy set, and there's something back that we don't know."

"What could they do?" put in Jud. "There's no more ferries."

"But there's a bridge," said I.

Ump, standing stock still in the floor, stumbled like a horse struck over the knees. Jud bolted out of the house on a dead run. We followed him to the stable, Ump galloping like a great rabbit.

We flung open the stable door, thrust the bits into the horses' mouths, and slapped on our saddles. It was murky, but we needed no light for business like this. We knew every part of the horse as a man knows his face, and we knew every strap and buckle.

Ump sat on his mare, waiting until we should be ready, kicking his stirrups with impatience, but his tongue, strangely enough, quiet. He turned his mare across the road before us when we were in our saddles.

"Jud," he said, "don't go off half-cocked. An' if there's hell raised, look out for Quiller. I'll stay here an' bring up the cattle as soon as it's light." Then he pulled his mare out of the way. El Mahdi was on his hind legs while Ump was speaking. When the Bay Eagle turned out, he came down with a great jump and began to run.

I bent over and clamped my knees to the horse and let him go. He was like some engine whose throttle is thrown open. In the first few plunges he seemed to rock with energy, as though he might be thrown off his legs by the pent-up driving-power. He and one other horse, the Black Abbot, started like this when they were mad. And, clinging in the saddle, one felt for a moment that the horse under him would rise out of the road or go crashing into the fence.

You will not understand this, my masters, if you have ridden only trained running horses or light hunters. They go about the business of a race with eagerness enough, but still as a servant goes about his task. Imagine, if you please, how a horse would run with you in the night if he was seventeen hands high and a barbarian!

We passed the tavern in a dozen plunges. I saw the candle which Ump had flung down, flickering by the horse-block, a little patch of light. Then the Cardinal's shoe crushed it out.

My coat sleeves cracked like sails. The wind seemed to whistle along my ribs. The horse's shoulders felt like pistons working under a cloth. I was a part of that horse. I fitted my body to him. I adjusted myself to the drive of his legs, to the rise and fall of his shoulders, to the play of every muscle. I rode when his back rocked, like a sort of loose hump fastened on it. His mane blew over my face and went streaming back. My nostrils were filled with the steam from his sweating skin.

Jud rode after the same manner, reducing the area of wind resistance to the smallest space. One watching the horses pass would have seen no rider at all. He might have marked a heavy outline as though something were bound across the saddle or clung flat to it.

You, my masters, who are accustomed to the horse as a slave, cannot know him as a freeman. That docked thing standing by the curb is a long bred-out degenerate. In the Hills a horse was born and bred up to be a freeman. When the time came, he yielded to a sort of human suzerainty, but he yielded as a cadet of a noble house yields to the discipline of a commandant, with the spirit in him and as one who condescended.

There were certain traditions which these horses seemed to hold. The Bay Eagle would never wear harness, nor would any of her blood, to the last one. The Black Abbot would never carry a woman's saddle, nor would his father nor his father's father. I have seen them fight like barbarian kings, great, tawny, desperate savages, bursting the straps and buckles as Samson burst the withes of the Philistines, fighting to kill, fighting to tear in pieces and destroy, fighting as a man fights when his standards are all down and he has lost a kingdom.

The earth was grey, with a few stars above it. The moon had gone over the mountains to make it day in the mystic city of Zeus, and the sun was still lagging along the other side of the world.

We thundered by the old weaver's little house squatting by the roadside, shut up tight like a sleeping eye. Then we swung down into the sandy strip of bottom leading to the bridge. The river was not a quarter of a mile away.

I began to pull on the bridle-reins. El Mahdi held the bit clamped in his teeth. I shifted a rein into each hand and tried to saw the bit loose, but I could not do it. Then, lying down on the saddle, I wound the slack of the reins around my wrists, caught out as far as I could, braced myself against the horn, and jerked with all the strength of my arms.

I jammed the tree of the saddle up on the horse's withers, but the bit held in his jaws. I knew then that the horse was running away. The devil seemed to be in him. He started in a fury, and he had run with a sort of rocking that ought to have warned me. I twisted my head around to look for Jud.

He had begun to pull up the Cardinal and had fallen a little behind, but he understood at once, shook out his reins, and leaned over in his saddle. The nose of the Cardinal came almost to my knee and hung there. Jud caught at my bridle, but he could not reach it. I wedged my knees against the leather pads of the saddle skirts, caught one side of the bridle-rein with both hands, and tried to throw the horse into the fence. I felt the leather of the rein stretch.

Then I knew that it was no use to try any further. Even if Jud could reach my bridle, he would merely tear it off at the bit-rings, and not stop the horse.

In a dozen seconds we would reach the stone abutment and go over into the river. I had no doubt that the bridge was down, or, if not, that its flooring was torn up.

I realised suddenly that it was my turn to go out of the world. I had seen people going out as though their turn came in a curious order, not unlike games which children play. But somehow I never thought that my turn would come. I was not really in that game. I was looking on when my name was called out.

El Mahdi struck the stone abutment and the bridge loomed. I dropped the reins and clung to the saddle, expecting the horse to fall with his legs broken, drive me against the sleepers and crash through.

We went on to the bridge like a rattle of musketry and thundered across. Horses, resembling women, as I have heard it said, are sometimes diverted from their purpose by the removal of every jot of opposition. With the reins on his neck, El Mahdi stopped at the top of the hill and I climbed down to the ground. My legs felt weak and I held on to the stirrup leather.

Jud dismounted, seized my bit, and ran his hand over El Mahdi's face. "I can't make head nor tail of that runnin'," he said. "He ain't scared nor he ain't mad."

"You couldn't tell with him," I answered.

"There never was a scared horse," responded Jud, "that wasn't nervous, an' there never was a mad one that wasn't hot. But this feller feels like a suckin' calf. It must have been devilment, an' he ought to be whaled."

"It wouldn't do any good," said I; "he'd only fight you and try to kill you."

"He's a dam' curious whelp," said Jud. "He must a knowed that the bridge was all right."

"How could he have known?" said I.

"They say," replied Jud, "that horses an' cattle sees things that folks don't see, an' that they know about what's goin' to happen. It's powerful curious about the things they do know."

We slipped the reins over the horses' heads and walked back to the bridge. Jud went on with his talking.

"Now, you can't get a horse on to a dangerous bridge, to save your life, an' you can't get him on ice that ain't strong enough to hold him, an' you can't get him to eat anything that'll hurt him, an' you can't get him lost. An' old Clabe says there's Bible for it that a horse can see spooks. I tell you, Quiller, El Mahdi knowed about that bridge."

Deep in my youthful bosom I was convinced that El Mahdi knew. But I put it wholly on the ground that he was a genius.

We crossed the river, led the horses down to the end of the abutment, and tied them to a fence. Then we went back and examined the bridge as well as we could in the dark. It stood over the river as the early men and Dwarfs had built it,—solid as a wall.

Woodford had given the thing up, and the road was open to the north country.

We sat down on the corner of the abutment near the horses, to wait for the daylight, Jud wearing old Christian's cap, and I bareheaded. We sat for a long time, listening to the choke and snarl of the water as it crowded along under the bridge.

Then we fell to a sort of whispering talk.

"Quiller," he began, "do you believe that story about the Dwarfs buildin' the bridge?"

"Ump don't," I answered. "Ump says it's a cock-and-bull story, and there never were any Dwarfs except once in a while a bad job like him."

"You can't take Ump for it," said he. "Ump won't believe anything he can't put his finger on, if it's swore to on a stack of Bibles. Quiller, I've seen them holes in the mountains where the Dwarfs lived, with the marks on the rocks like's on them logs, an' I've seen the rigamajigs that they cut in the sandstone. They could a built the bridge, if they took a notion, just by sayin' words."

He was quiet a while, and then he added, "An' I've seen the path where they used to come down to the river, an' it has places wore in the solid rock like you'd make with your big toe."

Jud stopped, and I moved up a little closer to him. I could see the ugly, crooked men crawl out of their caves and come sneaking down from the mountains to strangle the sleeping and burn the roof. I could see their twisted bare feet, their huge, slack mouths, and their long hands that hung below their knees when they walked. And then, on the hill beyond the Valley River, I heard a sound.

I seized my companion by the arm. "Jud," I said under my breath, "did you hear that?"

He leaned over me and listened. The sound was a sort of echo.

"They're comin'," he whispered.

"The Dwarfs?" said I.

"Lem Marks," said he.

# CHAPTER XX
# ON THE ART OF GOING TO RUIN

The sound reached the summit of the hill, and then we heard it clearly,—the ringing of horseshoes on the hard road. They came in a long trot, clattering into the little hollow at the foot of the abutment to the bridge. We heard men dismounting, horses being tied to the fence, and a humming of low talk. We listened, lying flat beside El Mahdi and the Cardinal.

It was difficult to determine how many were in the hollow, but all were now afoot but one. We could hear his horse tramping, and hear him speaking to the others from the saddle above them.

A man with his back toward us lighted a lantern. When he turned to lead the way up the abutment into the bridge, we caught a flickering picture of the group. I could make out Lem Marks as the man with the lantern, and Malan behind him, and I could see the brown shoulder of the horse and the legs of the rider, but the man's face was above the reach of the light. It was perhaps Parson Peppers.

They stopped at the sill of the bridge, and the man with the lantern began to examine the flooring and the ends of the logs set into the stone of the abutment.

He moved about slowly, holding the lantern close to the ground. Malan stopped by the horse. I could see the dingy light now moving in the bridge, now held over the edge of the abutment, now creeping along the borders of the sill.

Once it passed close to the horse, and I saw his hoofs clearly and his brown legs, and the club feet of Malán, and the gleam of an axe. They were on the far side of the river, and the howling of the water tumbled their voices into a sort of jumble. The man on the horse seemed to give some directions which were carried out by the one with the lantern. Then they gathered in a little group and put the thing under discussion.

Lem Marks talked for some minutes, and once Malan pointed with the axe. I could see the light slip along its edge. Then they all went into the bridge together.

The tallow candle struggling through the dingy windows of the lantern lighted the bridge as a dying fire lights a forest, in a little space, half-heartedly, with all the world blacker beyond that space. They stopped at the bridge-mouth on our side of the river, and Marks carried the lantern over the lower end of the abutment. Then he called Malan. The clubfoot got down on his knees and held the light over by the log sleeper of the bridge.

I could see where the bark had been burned along the log. I heard Marks say that this was the place to cut. Then the man on the horse rode out close to Malan and bent over to look. The clubfoot raised his lantern, and the rider's face came into the play of the light. My heart lifted trembling into my throat. It was Woodford!

I grabbed for Jud, and my fingers caught the knee of his breeches. He was squatted down in the road with a stone in his hand.

Woodford nodded his head, gave some order which I could not hear, and moved his horse back from the edge of the abutment. Malan arose and picked up his axe. Marks took the lantern, trying to find some place where the light could be thrown on the face of the log. He shifted to several positions and finally took a place at the corner of the bridge, holding the light over the side.

Malan stood with his club feet planted wide on the log, leaned over, and began to hack the bark off where he wished to take out his great chip.

I could hear the little pieces of charred bark go rattling down into the river. Malan notched the borders of his chip, then shifted his weight a little to his right leg and swung the axe back over his shoulder. It came down gleaming true, it seemed to me, but the blade, turning as it descended, dealt the log a glancing blow and wrenched the handle out of the man's hand. I saw the axe glitter as it passed the smoked glass of the lantern. Then it struck the side of the bridge with a great ripping bang, and dropped into the river.

I jumped up with a cry of "the Dwarfs!"

The swing of the axe carried Malan forward. He lost his balance, threw up his hands and began to topple. I saw the shadow of the horse fall swiftly across the light. Malan was seized by the collar and flung violently backward. Then Woodford caught the lantern from Marks and came on down the abutment toward us.

He rode slowly with the lantern against his knee. The horse, blinded by the light, did not see us until he was almost upon us. Then he jumped back with a snort. Woodford raised the lantern above his head and looked down.

Bareheaded, in Roy's roundabout, I was a queer looking youngster. Jud, with old Christian's leather cap pulled on his head and a stone in his fist, might have been brother to any cutthroat. Stumbled upon in the dark we must have looked pretty wild.

Woodford regarded us with very apparent unconcern. "Quiller," he said, as one might have announced a guest of indifferent welcome. Then he set the lantern down on his saddle horn. "Well," he said, "this is a piece of luck."

I was struck dumb by the man's friendly voice and my resolution went to pieces. I began to stammer like a novice taken in a wrong. Then Woodford did a cunning thing.

He assumed that I was not embarrassed, but that I was amused at his queer words.

"Upon my life, Quiller," he said, "I don't wonder that you laugh. It was a queer thing to go blurting out, you moving the very devil to get your cattle over the Valley, and I using every influence I may have with that gentleman to prevent it. Now, that was a funny speech."

I got my voice then. "I don't see the luck of it," I said.

"And that," said he, "is just what I am about to explain. In the meantime Jud might toss that rock into the river." There was a smile playing on the man's face.

"If it's the same to you," said Jud, "I'll just hold on to the rock."

"As you please," replied Woodford, still smiling down at me. "I'd like a word with you, Quiller. Shall we go out on the road a little?"

"Not a foot," said I.

On my life, the man sighed deeply and passed his hand over his face. "If I had such men," he said, "I wouldn't be here pulling down a bridge. Your brother, Quiller, is in great luck. With such men, I could twist the cattle business around my finger. But when one has to depend upon a lot of numbskulls, he can expect to come out at the little end of the horn."

I began to see that this Woodford, under some lights, might be a very sensible and a very pleasant man. He got down from his saddle, held up the lantern and looked me over. Then he set the light on the ground and put his hands behind his back. "Quiller," he began, as one speaks into a sympathetic ear, "there is no cement that will hold a man to you unless it is blood wetted. You can buy men by the acre, but they are eye servants to the last one. A brother sticks, right or wrong, and perhaps a son sticks, but the devil take the others. I never had a brother, and, therefore, Providence put me into the fight one arm short."

He began to walk up and down behind the lantern, taking a few long strides and then turning sharply. "Doing things for one's self," he went on, "comes to be tiresome business. A man must have someone to work for, or he gets to the place where he doesn't care." He stopped before me with his face full in the light. "Quiller," he said, and the voice seemed to ring true, "I meant to prevent your getting north with these cattle. I hoped to stop you without being compelled to destroy this bridge, but you force me to make this move, and I shall make it. Still, on my life, I care so little that I would let the whole thing go on the spin of a coin."

His face brightened as though the idea offered some easy escape from an unpleasant duty. "Upon my word," he laughed, "I was not intending to be so fair. But the offer is out, and I will stand by it."

He put his hand in his pocket and took out a silver dollar. "You may toss, Quiller, heads or tails as you choose."

I refused, and the man pitched the coin into the air, caught it in his hand and returned it to his pocket.

"Perhaps you think you will be able to stop me," he said in a voice that came ringing over something in his throat. "We're three, and Malan is a better man than Jud."

"He is not a better man," said I.

"There is a way to tell," said he.

"And it can't begin too quick," said I.

"Done," said he. "At it they go, right here in the road, and the devil take me if Malan does not dust your man's back for you."

He spun around, caught up the lantern, and we all went up to the level floor of the abutment at the bridge sill. Lem Marks and the clubfoot were waiting. Woodford turned to them.

"Malan," he said, "I've heard a great deal of talk out of you about a wrestle with Jud at Roy's tavern. Now I'm going to see if there's any stomach behind that talk."

I thrust in. "It must be fair," I said.

"Fair it shall be," said he; "catch-as-catch-can or back-holds?" And he turned to Malan.

"Back-holds," said the clubfoot, "if that suits Jud."

"Anything suits me," answered Jud.

The two men stripped. Jud asked for the lantern and examined the ground. It was the width of the abutment, perhaps thirty feet, practically level, and covered with a loose sand dust. There was no railing to this abutment, not even a coping along its borders.

I followed Jud as he went over every foot of the place. I wanted to ask him what he thought, but I was afraid. Presently he came back to the bridge, set down the lantern, and announced that he was ready.

There was not a breath of air moving. The door of the lantern stood open, and the smoke from the half-burned tallow candle streamed straight up and squeezed out at the peaked top.

The two men took their places, leaned over, and each put his big arms around the other. Malan had torn the sleeves out of his shirt, and Jud had rolled his above the elbow.

Woodford picked up the lantern, nodded to me to follow him, and we went around the men to see if the positions they had taken were fair. Each was entitled to one underhold, that is, the right arm around the body and under the left arm of his opponent, the left arm over the opponent's right, and the hands gripped. It is the position of the grizzly, hopeless for the weaker man.

The two had taken practically the same hold, except that Malan locked his fingers, while Jud gripped his left wrist with his right hand. Jud was perhaps four inches taller, but Malan was heavier by at least twenty pounds.

We came back and stood by the floor of the bridge, Woodford holding the lantern with Lem Marks and I beside him. Malan said that the light was in his eyes, and Woodford shifted the lantern until the men's faces were in the dark. Then he gave the word.

For fully a minute, it seemed to me, the two men stood, like a big bronze. Then I could see the muscles of their shoulders contracting under a powerful tension as though each were striving to lift some heavy thing up out of the earth. It seemed, too, that Malan squeezed as he lifted, and that Jud's shoulder turned a little, as though he wished to brace it against the clubfoot's breast, or was troubled by the squeezing.

Malan bent slowly backward, and Jud's heels began to rise out of the dust. Then, as though a crushing weight descended suddenly through his shoulder, Jud threw himself heavily against Malan, and the two fell. I ran forward, the men were down sidewise in the road.

"Dog fall," said Woodford; "get up."

But the blood of the two was now heated. They hugged, panted, and rolled over. Woodford thrust the lantern into their faces and began to kick Malan. "Get up, you dog," he said.

They finally unlocked their arms and got slowly on their legs. Both were breathing deeply and the sweat was trickling over their faces.

Woodford looked at the infuriated men and seemed to reflect. Presently he turned to me, as the host turns to the honourable guest. "Quiller," he said, "these savages want to kill each other. We shall have to close the Olympic games. Let us say that you have won, and no tales told. Is it fair?"

I stammered that it was fair. Then he came over and linked his arm through mine. He asked me if I would walk to the horses with him. I could not get away, and so I walked with him.

He pointed to the daylight breaking along the edges of the hills, and to the frost glistening on the bridge roof. He said it reminded him how, when he was little, he would stand before the frosted window panes trying to understand what the etched pictures meant, and how sure he was that he had once known about this business, but had somehow forgotten. And how he tried and tried to recall the lost secret. How sometimes he seemed about to get it, and then it slipped away, and how one day he realised that he should never remember, and what a blow it was.

Then he said a lot of things that I did not understand. He said that when one grew out of childhood, he lost his sympathy with events, and when that sympathy was lost, it was possible to live in the world only as an adventurer with everything in one's hand.

He said a sentinel watched to see if a man set his heart on a thing, and if he did the sentinel gave some sign, whereupon the devil's imps swarmed up to break that thing in pieces. He said that sometimes a man beat off the devils and saved the thing, but it was rare, and meant a life of tireless watching. From every point of view, indifference was better.

Still, he said, it was a mistake for a man to allow events to browbeat him. He ought to fight back, hitting where he could. An event, once in a while, was strangely a coward. Besides that, if Destiny found a man always ready to strip, she came after a while to accord to him the courtesies of a duellist, and if he were a stout fellow, she sometimes hesitated before she provoked a fight. Of course the man could not finally beat her off, but she would set him to one side, as a person with whom she was going to have trouble, and give him all the time she could.

He said a man ought to have the courage to strike out for what he wanted; that the ship-wrecked who got desperately ashore was a better man than the hanger-back; that a great misfortune was a great compliment. It measured the resistance of the man. Destiny would not send artillery against a weakling. It was sometimes finer to fight when the lights were all out; I would not understand that, men never did until they were about through with life. But, above everything else, he said, a man ought to go to his ruin with a sort of princely indifference. God Almighty could not hurt the man who did not care.

Then he gave me a friendly direction about the cattle, to put them in his boundary on our road home, bade me remember our contract of no tales told, and got into his saddle.

I watched him cross the bridge, and ride away through the Hills with his men, humming some song about the devil and a dainty maid, and I wished that I might grow up to have such splendid courage. His big galleon had gone down on the high seas with a treasure in her hold that I could not reckon, and he went singing like one who finds a kingdom.

Then Jud called to me to get out of the road, and a muley steer went by at my elbow.

# CHAPTER XXI
# THE EXIT OF THE PRETENDER

I sat in the saddle of El Mahdi on the hill-top beyond the bridge, and watched the day coming through the gateway of the world. It was a work of huge enchantment, as when, for the pleasure of some ancient caliph, or at the taunting of some wanton queen, a withered magus turned the ugly world into a kingdom of the fairy, and the lolling hangers-on started up on their elbows to see a green field spreading through the dirty city and great trees rising above the vanished temples, and wild roses and the sweet dew-drenched brier trailing where the camel's track had just faded out, and autumn leaves strewn along pathways of a wood, and hills behind it all where the sunlight flooded.

It was like the mornings that came up from the sea by the Wood Wonderful, or those that broke smiling when the world was newly minted,—mornings that trouble the blood of the old shipwreck sunning by the door, and move the stay-at-home to sail out for the Cloud Islands. Full of the joy of life was this October land.

I could almost hear the sunlight running with a shout as it plunged in among the hickory trees and went tumbling to the thickets of the hollow. The mist hanging over the low meadows was a golden web, stretched by enchanted fingers across some exquisite country into which a man might come only through his dreams.

I waited while the drove went by, counting the cattle to see that none had been overlooked in the night. The Aberdeen-Angus still held his place in the front, and the big muley bull marched by like a king's governor, keeping his space of clear road at the peril of a Homeric struggle.

I knew every one of the six hundred, and I could have hugged each great black fellow as he trudged past.

Jud and the Cardinal went by in the middle of the long line and passed out of sight behind a turn of the hill below. The giant rode slowly, lolling in his saddle and swinging his big legs free of the stirrups.

Then the lagging rear of the drove trailed up, and the hunchback followed on the Bay Eagle. He was buttoned to the chin in Roy's blue coat and looked for all the world like some shrivelled old marshal of the empire, a hundred days out of Paris, covering the retreat of the imperial army.

El Mahdi stood on the high bank by the roadside, in among the dead blackberry briers, and I sat with the rein under my legs and my hands in my pockets.

The hunchback stopped his horse in the road below me, squared himself in his saddle, and looked up with a great supercilious grin.

"Well," he said, "I'll be damn!"

"What's the trouble?" said I.

"Humph!" he snorted, "are them britches I see on your legs?"

"That's what they call them," said I.

"Well," said he, "when you git home, take 'em off, an' hand 'em over to old Liza, an' ask her to bring your kilts down out of the garret. For you're as innocent a little codger as ever sucked his hide full of milk."

"What are you driving at?" I asked.

Ump shook out his long arms and folded them around the bosom of his blue coat. "Jud told me," he said; "an' the pair of you ought to be put in a cradle with a rock-a-by-baby. Woodford was done when that axe fell in the river, an' he knowed it. He was ridin' out when he saw you an' Jud, an' he said to himself, 'God's good to you, Rufus, my boy; here's a pair of little babies a long way from their ma, an' it ought to count you one.' Then he lit off an' offered to wrastle you, heads I win an' tails you lose, for the cake in your pocket, an' then he chucked you under the chin, an' you promised not to tell."

The hunchback set his two fingers against his teeth and whistled like a hawk, a long, shrill, hissing whistle that startled the little partridges on the sloping hillside and sent them scurrying under the dead grass, and brought the drumming pheasant to his feathered legs.

Then he threw his chin into the air and squinted. "Quiller," he piped, with the long echo still whining in his throat, "that whistle fooled you an' it fooled Jud, but it wouldn't fool a Bob White with the shell on its back. When the old bird hears it, she don't wait to see the long shadow travellin' on the grass, but she hollers, 'Into the weeds, boys, if you want to save your bacon.' An' you ought to see the little codgers scatter. Let it be a lesson to you,

Quiller, my laddiebuck; when you hear that whistle, light out for the tall timber. When you're a fightin' the devil, half the winnin' 's in the runnin'."

Then he opened his great cavernous mouth and began to bellow,

> "Ho! ho! for the carrion crow,
> But hark to the sqawk of the carrion hawk,"

gathered up his reins and set out after the drove in a hand gallop, all doubled over in his blue coat.

I got El Mahdi into the road and we went swinging down the hill. I had a light flashed into the deeps of Woodford, and I saw dimly how able and how dangerous a man he was. I began to comprehend something of the long complex formula that goes to make up a human identity, and it was a discovery as startling as when a fellow perched on his grandfather's shoulder sees through the key-hole a tangle of wheels all going behind the white face of the clock.

I had been deftly handled by this Woodford, and yet I had not seemed to be. He had striven to move me to his will with a sort of masked edging, and, failing in that, left me with the bitterness drawn out. More than that,—shrewd and far-sighted man,—taken hot against him, I was almost won over to his star.

Under the hammering of the hard-headed Ump, I saw Woodford in another light. But I carried no ill will. He had jousted hard and lost, and youth holds no post-mortems. But the flock of night birds had not flown out into the sun. Dislodged from one quarter, they flapped across my heart to another ridgepole.

Woodford had been holding the blue hills with his men, and we knew what it meant to go up against him. But down yonder in among the Lares of our house, one worked against us with her nimble fingers. My heart went hard against the woman.

If she drew back from our floorboard, there was the tongue in her head to say it. No obligation bound her. True, we had given her of our love freely. But it was a thing no man could set a price on, and no man could pay, save as he told back the coin which he had borrowed. And failing in that coin, it was a debt beyond him.

The door to our house stood pulled back on its hinges. Nothing barred it but the sun. If the god Whim was piping, she could follow to the world's end. One might as well bow out the woman when her blood is cooling. Against the human heart the king's writs have never run.

I slapped my pocket above the letter. The current had turned and was running landward. The evil thing cast out upon its flood was riding back. I hoped it might sting cruelly the hand that flung it.

I rose in my stirrups and shook my youthful fists at the hills beyond the Gauley. I could see the smile dying on her red mouth when one came to say that her plans were ship-wrecked.

Then I thought of Ward, and something fluttered in my throat. He was under the spell of this slim, brown-haired witch. She was in his blood, running to his finger-tips. She was on him like the sun. Why could not the woman see what the good God was handing down to her? It was the treasure worth a kingdom. Did she think to find this thing at any crossroads? Oh, she would see. She would see. This thing was found rarely by the luckiest, so rarely that many an old wise man held that there was no such treasure under the sun, and the quest of it was but a fool's errand.

I was a mile behind the drove, and when I came up it had reached the borders of Woodford's land. Jud had thrown down the high fence, staked-and-ridered with long chestnut rails, and the stream of cattle was pouring through and spreading out over the great pasture. I watched the little groups of muleys strike out through the deep broom-sedge hollows and the narrow bulrush marshes and the low gaps of the good sodded hills, spying this new country, finding where the grass was sweetest and where the water bubbled in the old poplar trough, and what wind-sheltered cove would be warmest to a fellow's belly when he lay sleeping in the sun.

Then we rode north through the Hills, over the Gauley where the oak leaves carpeted the ford, and the little trout darted like a beam of light, and the old fish-hawk sat on the hanging limb of the dead beech-tree with his shoulders to his ears and his beak drooping, like some worn-out voluptuary brooding on his sins.

On we went through the deep wooded lanes where the redbird stepped about in his long crimson coat, jerring at the wren, who worked in the deep thicket as though the Master Builder had gone away to kingdom come and left her behind to finish the world.

We came to many a familiar landmark of my golden babyhood, the enchanted grove on the Seely Hill where I had hunted fabled monsters and gone whooping down among the cattle, the Greathouse meadow where Red Mike pitched me out of the saddle when he grew tired of having his bit jerked, and I sat up in my little petticoats and solemnly demanded that

Jourdan should cut his head off, a thing the old man promised on his sacred honour when he could borrow the ax of the man in the moon; the high gate-post by the cattle-scales where I perched bareheaded in a calico dress and watched old Bedford make his last fight against human government, Bedford, a bull of mysterious notions, that would kill you if he found you walking in his field, and lick your stirrup if you came riding on a horse.

It was now a country of rich meadow-land, and blue-grass hills rising to long, flat ridges that the hickories skirted; but in that other time it was a land of wonders, where in any summer morning, if a fellow set out on his chubby legs, he might come to enchanted forests, lost rivers, halcyon kingdoms guarded by some spell where the roving fairies hunted the great bumblebee to the doorway of his house, and slew him on its sill and carried off his treasure.

Through the fringe of locust bushes along the roadside we caught the first glimpse of home, and the three horses pricked up their ears and swung out in a longer trot. We clattered down the wide lane and tumbled out of the saddles at the gate, leaving the Bay Eagle standing proudly like some victorious general, and the Cardinal like a tired giant who has done his work, and El Mahdi with his grey head high above the gate looking away as of old to the far-off mountains as though he wondered vaguely if the friend or the message or the enemy would never come.

We marched over the flagstone walk and into the house and up the stairway. Old Liza flung us some warning through a window to the garden, which we failed to catch and bellowed back a welcome. Then we gained the door to the library, threw it open and went crowding in.

A step beyond that door we halted with a jerk. Ward was lounging in a big chair with a pillow behind his shoulder, and over by the open window where the sun danced along the casement was Cynthia Carper setting a sheaf of roses in a jar.

Ward looked us down to the floor, and then he laughed until the great chair tottered on its legs. "Cynthia," he cried, "will you drop a courtesy to the gallant troopers?" She spun around with a fear kindling in her eyes.

"The cattle!" she said. "Did you get them over?"

I had the situation in my fingers, and I felt myself grow taller with it. "Yes," I said harshly. Then I put my hand into my pocket, drew out the letter and handed it to her with a mocking bow. "I was asked to carry this letter back to you, and say that my brother's word is good enough for Nicholas Marsh."

She took the envelope and stood twisting it in her slim fingers, while a light came up slowly in the land beyond her eyelids.

Ward held out his hand for the letter. And then I looked to see her flutter like a pinned fly. She grew neither red nor white, but crossed to his chair and put the letter in his hand.

He tore off the envelope and ran his eyes down the written page. "Your order for the money!" he cried; "this was not mentioned in our plan. What is this?"

"That," said the straight young woman, "is a field order of the commanding general issued without the knowledge of the war department."

Then I saw the whole underpinning of the scheme, and my heart stumbled and went groping about the four walls of its house. I tramped out of the room and down the stairway to the big window at the first landing. I stopped and leaned out over the walnut casement. El Mahdi stood as I had left him, staring at the far-off wall of the Hills; and below me in the garden old Liza stooped over her vines, not a day older, it seemed to me, than when I galloped at her long apron-strings on Alhambra the Son of the Wind.